MW01639570

HOME FOR GOOD

Gerald James Avila

Tony Salvador, Photographer

Abbott Press books may be ordered through booksellers or by contacting:

Abbott Press
1663 Liberty Drive
Bloomington, IN 47403
www.abbottpress.com
Phone: 1 (866) 697-5310

ISBN: 978-1-4582-2012-7 (sc)
ISBN: 978-1-4582-2013-4 (e)

Library of Congress Control Number: 2016905159

Print information available on the last page.

Abbott Press rev. date: 5/17/2016

TONY SALVADOR

June 9, 1949 - March 12, 2014

I dedicate my book “Home for Good” to the late Tony Salvador. His photographs for my first two book covers would not have been possible without his expertise. Some people in life just seem to make things easier for others. Tony did that for me. My third book cover is going to be without him, unless God gives him permission to work in a spiritual way. I’ll be listening for the way.

ACKNOWLEDGEMENTS

My editor: *Lance Knight*, for a job very well done.
My wife: *Arlene*, for putting up with my characters who live in my head, and seem to surface when we are having a conversation, and also her constant thoughts on book promoting.
My proof readers: *Cece Short*, who has probably read more books than all the words I have put to paper. And *Darlene Graham*, who gave me a lot of encouragement.
My mother-n-law: *Evangeline Rose*, who is not afraid to tell it like she sees it.
My son: *Jake Avila*, for reading about my characters and all their shortcomings.
My daughter: *Jennifer*, in helping my incompetence on the computer.
My wife's assistant: *Fernanda Mendes*, who is more like a business partner with her many skills. She is Amazing

...And to all of you who like to read,
and those who want to read,
starting now.

CHAPTER 1

"Damn-it! I just can't do this anymore. When am I going to write more than one stupid sentence on a sheet of paper?" Jeffrey ripped the sheet of paper from the typewriter, wadded it with total disgust, and threw it at the wastebasket with the velocity of a fastball. The wads were piling up. Most of them had missed the intended target, leaving a mess of crumpled papers around the wastebasket near the window. Next to his fast food left overs on the filing cabinet there were some Chinese noodles in a box, along with remnants of stained paper from the hamburgers and fries of his last two meals. It was all beginning to smell like an alley dumpster outside a restaurant.

"God, what is wrong with me?" Jeff looked up at the crucifix his wife had hung over the writing room door, years before. He took a deep breath, sighed and slipped another piece of paper into the typewriter. Jeff was old school, with his trusted typewriter. He refused to graduate to a computer, fearing a change of writing tools could hamper his success. At wits end, he sat for a minute hoping to find his writing muse, then began to type a different sentence. Before he finished, he slammed the keys, jamming them in blind frustration. He jumped to his feet ripping out the paper in disgust, then suddenly paused... an impish smile split his face.

He went to the window, opened it, grabbed the typewriter off the desk and slung it out onto the grass that separated Alice Bates' house from his.

Hearing his shouts of rage and victory from next door, Alice opened her window to the chilly Connecticut morning and looked down at the smashed typewriter. "Jeff have you flipped out again?" Her loud voice momentarily caught him off guard. He shouted back, "Yes, and it feels so good to smash that worthless piece of crap."

"I'm coming over, Jeff. Don't throw anything else out the window." Still dressed in her pajamas, she slipped her robe on, and went out the back door. Crossing the yard, she quickly gathered her robe across her neck and chest against the cold wind, early signs that winter was coming. Knowing that Jeff had a bad habit of leaving his back door unlocked she went in, and straight into his writing room, she knew the house well. When her husband was alive, the four of them, *Jeff* and *Marilyn*, *Sam* and *Alice*, were inseparable. Their first year of friendship, they had fun comparing each other's looks in comparison to Hollywood stars. Marilyn was a dead ringer for Doris Day. Jeff looked remarkably like a young Clint Eastwood, except Jeff's eyes were so blue that they almost looked like he had tinted contacts. Alice resembled Meryl Streep, with hair color and build. Now Sam looked like no one they could think of, so they decided to make him the look-alike of Troy Donahue, because all four of them loved the movie "A Summer Place." In reality Sam was more like a character actor, with rugged features that made him like a hunk of steel that women found irresistible. They were the life of every party.

Sam had died nearly four years earlier. Alice and Marilyn became even closer after his untimely death; he crashed his Cessna 172 into the side a mountain during a snow storm, on the Catskills in upstate New York.

Alice told herself over and over that she should have been more insistent that he stay put, but he was anxious to head home. His work as a college employment representative for graduating seniors in Syracuse, New York, was done. After four long weeks away from home, he'd decided rather than stay over in Syracuse waiting for the storm to clear, he wanted to sleep in his own bed that night. She had pleaded with him to stay, but his mind was made up.

"One year later Marilyn was diagnosed with a brain tumor. Alice was there for both Marilyn and Jeff the next few months. She was a Godsend to them both. *Josh*, their twenty-two-year-old son, would come home from Rutgers on weekends. He'd sit next to her doing his school work, giving his mother pleasure just to be near him. Marilyn took a turn for the worse during the fourth month, nearing the end of her life. She lay on her deathbed with Jeff sitting next to her, holding her hand. Alice cleaned up in the kitchen, then brought Marilyn some broth. Jeff left for the kitchen, trying to find something, anything, to pull him out of depression. He went outside for some fresh of air.

Marilyn finally had her chance to speak with Alice alone. She asked her to sit beside her on the bed. Alice held her hand, wishing in her mind she could be the one God would take, and just leave Marilyn and Jeff to live a long and happy life together.

Marilyn, knowing she had only hours to live, struggled to speak clearly and loudly enough for Alice to hear her last wishes. She coughed, then whispered, "Alice, I want you and Jeff to get together." She gasped for air to finish her words. "The four of us got along so well all these years and it would seem natural for the two of you to end up as a couple." Marilyn's voice was fading, and turning raspy, leaving Alice straining to hear.

"You're talking nonsense, Marilyn, I'm not looking for someone else and I know Jeff won't be either."

"I don't mean right away," coughing to clear her voice to continue, "but just keep him in mind. Jeff is going to have it very hard, and I know you went through hell yourself when you lost Sam. So just keep him in mind, please?" Staring into Alice's eyes, she waited for an agreeing response.

"I will watch out for him, but your Jeff is just that, *your* Jeff."

"Alice," Marilyn gasping for enough air to keep talking, "I must… tell you… something, and I apologize for not…t-t-telling you sooner" … Too weak to speak anymore, she finally relinquished her thought, closing her eyes to sleep.

Marilyn passed the next morning.

When Alice made it to the study, she stopped and looked around the room. Then with a slight stutter, "J-Jeff, what kind of a mess is this? It looks and smells like a pigsty. If Marilyn were here she'd be so upset with you."

"But she isn't here, Alice"

"No, but I am, and she told me to watch out for you, so that's what I'm going to do, whether you like it or not."

Jeff gazed out the front window of his study, more calm now, "You know this was Marilyn's favorite time of year? That may seem strange because our daughter died this time of year. She always said that Jodie was nearest in this season."

He looked at the trees across the street; they were beginning to show their New England fall colors. His eyes teared up with thoughts of the trees. "Jodie had called out all the names of the trees she could see from this window.

"Her favorite was the Quaking Aspen because she could put her arms around the trunk and hug it. The White Oak, Sycamore, and Tulip trees were too large to hug.

It was the best time for all four of us. Our fall picnics and the golf challenges we had… and the Jazz Festival every year, and how crazy we'd act. It seemed that every year we'd get crazier. We were like four kids in high school. I was looking out this window when I saw you and Sam standing in the street admiring your new home. It was going to be your first night in it, on September 2, 1980," Jeff said.

Alice smiled, "How did you know we weren't saying 'My God, are we crazy buying this hundred-year-old house that needs work?'"

"Not with the cheery look you two had. I told Marilyn, I thought you'd be neighbors who would keep your house and yard neat and clean. I was only half right, because you also became very special to us," Jeff continued. "We needed each other."

She agreed, "Yes, it was our dream home. We looked everywhere for a place to live in the northeast, but then we drove into Litchfield. We were tired of looking and decided to drive down your street on our way to the freeway and out of town. But when we saw the 'for sale' sign, we both just knew we'd be setting down roots in the state of Connecticut… and how did you and Marilyn settle here? For all the years we've know each other, I've never known where you came from. I knew that Marilyn grew up in Missoula, Montana and graduated from the University of Montana, but after that I don't know how you two ended up here."

Jeff and Marilyn had both agreed that the past would be left unsaid and the two would look ahead and keep their memories private. Sam warned Alice not to snoop in their neighbors past, after playing golf with Jeff and discovering how sensitive he was to questions about their past, by clamming up.

"Are you doing some kind of therapy on me, Alice, because it sure sounds like it?" She commented quickly, "Partly, and partly I'm just curious to understand why you are like you are."

Jeff went on, "Whatever that means, good or bad, I'll tell you how we got here. I graduated from Rutgers University and moved to New York City, just like every wanna be writer did. To survive, you had to take editing jobs just to eat, and all the editing jobs were in New York. I wrote a number of articles and sold them for just enough to fill my sandwiches with bologna, instead of just bread and ketchup. When I completed my first short novella, I soon realized, the publisher was going to make most of the money from the book like, they did on the rest of my published short stories; and I would end up with a few pennies. So when I saw an advertisement in the New York Times that Rutgers was having a work shop on publishing, I jumped on the bus that weekend and headed over to Jersey." Alice sat down at Marilyn's desk, figuring this might take a while.

Jeff continued, "I was a few minutes late, but so what, it's not like we were getting a grade for attending. I was familiar with the campus, and even the room for the workshop, having had a literature class in that very room. In fact, I sat in the same chair as when I was in class. Just two rows from the top. It was always nice to sit up high and look down at the professors, sort of like you were not going to be intimidated by anyone. A few moments later, a very attractive woman came in from the side door at the top, and asked me if anybody was sitting in the seat next to me. I made a stupid crack and said, 'No, nobody is sitting here or there or there or there or even over there.' I have that tendency, when a woman has that physical attraction, of green eyes, brown shiny hair, my guard comes done. Much like you Alice, except your hair is blond."

"The woman mumbled her words." 'I am sorry, I'm a little nervous, I don't know anyone here and I wish I hadn't come.' "I felt so bad about making a smart-aleck joke to her that I invited her to have lunch at the break. When we got our sandwiches and a drink I insisted on paying for both. The total was eight dollars and change. The cash register lady gave me my three cents change. I looked at the three cents with a smile then looked at the cashier." She shrugged her shoulders apathetically. "That was all the money I had until my check on Monday the fifteenth."

"We sat down to eat and the first thing she asked was, 'Are you broke?' I insisted I wasn't. When the seminar was over she stretched out her hand and said, 'Hold my hand and don't lose me, I'm your ticket home to New York.' "We discovered, we only lived eight blocks from each other. From that day on we never missed a day seeing each other, for at least a few minutes. A short time later I sold my short novel to Mayhill Publishing House. I insisted on paying her rent until she sold her first children's book. She reluctantly agreed.

"We shared our writing styles with each other, which meant spending a lot of time together. One afternoon we went to Central Park to observe people and take notes on how they interact. We were always studying how people handled everyday living so we'd have material to write. Out of the blue, I asked her what the mascot was at the University of Montana. She responded, without hesitation, 'It's a *Grizzly Bear*.' She asked about the Rutgers mascot, and I proudly said, Scarlet Knight. She began to laugh like I had told the funniest joke ever, making the comment that a little red knight would be wiped out by the grizzly in a second. She started to apologize thinking she hurt my feelings until I began to laugh…

We sat on a bench near that famous footbridge, the one movies always have in their films where the bad guys are being chased by the cops, then Marilyn asked me to marry her. I said, "Yes, but shouldn't I be the one asking you?" She said, 'You may.' I said, "Marilyn Dunne, will you marry me?" She responded, 'To know you is to love you. I certainly will Jeffrey Williams.' I said, "I think you stole that line from a movie." She laughed and declared it was her line now. We went to Missoula, told her parents, and got married in a church off West Broadway St., just blocks from the Missoula cemetery."

"Oh! That was the same church that you had services for her?"

"Yes. She always told me that church would be her last Mass. She often spoke of death, but she wasn't a fatalist. She knew she had allergic reactions to penicillin and other medications. That gave her concerns about paramedics making a mistake by giving her penicillin or something else that would take her life if she had a car accident. That was why she wore her Medic Alert bracelet all the time." Alice looked down at Jeff's wrist and he said, "Yes, I also wear a bracelet for my allergic reaction to bee stings. I am so glad that Josh doesn't seem to have any allergies."

"Her whole family is buried at the Missoula Cemetery. She always said, knowing she would be buried there made her feel like she would be home someday. But that's not the only reason she said that. We moved a lot the first five years of our marriage and it was not fun. So when the topic came up about whether she wanted to be buried in Missoula if she should die suddenly, she said that would be her home for good."

"I saw your daughter's tombstone next to where Marilyn was being buried… It just dawned on me why you remembered the exact day when Sam and I moved here. It was your daughter Jodie's, birthday. I didn't even remember the exact day we moved in until now. Marilyn seldom talked about Jodie without crying, so I left it alone. I felt she would talk about it, if or when she was ready," Alice observed.

Tears started streaming down his face as he proceeded, "Jodie was so smart. I asked her one day, when she was 5, what she was writing on her note pad. She was sitting at my desk mimicking me." Jeff looked at his desk as though he could see her. Her response was, 'Daddy, I'm starting my novel.' 'That's very good Jodie, how far have you gotten?' 'I've done my first paragraph. You know what a paragraph is?' Jodie answered with pride, 'Yes. It's a bunch of sentences together.' Jeff pointed to those framed words hanging on the wall above the book cabinet, "I was even surprised she knew what a sentence was. She died in a school bus going to her elementary school in Stamford that fall. Three kids were killed. The man who rammed the bus was high on drugs… he also died. Jodie was six and Josh was two. She would be twenty-six now." The loss of both Marilyn and Jodie was forever haunting his mind. He needed Josh more than anything in the world, just to keep him sane.

Alice had heard about the tragedy, years earlier, from Marilyn, but only occasionally, and only in bits and pieces. It was getting close to Jodie's birthday as the end of summer was nearing. Marilyn felt a special closeness, before and after Jodie's birthday. It was spiritual in her mind.

"I found myself fearing every time Marilyn was planning to take Josh anywhere in the car, Jeff almost whispered. When you two moved in, I began golfing with Sam. I'm sure Sam told you how paranoid I was."

Alice said, "Sam once told me how nervous you became when you knew that Marilyn and Josh would be leaving to go shopping in downtown Torrington, while you two were golfing… and before you two could finish 9 holes your shirt would be wringing wet."

Jeff said thoughtfully, "It wasn't just once, it was time after time. Finally, I just said to myself, 'It's in God's hands.' Things started getting a little better after that."

"We were living in the suburbs of Stamford, Connecticut at that time. Neither of us could handle big city life any longer, so we shopped around for a rural place to live. When we drove into Litchfield to eat, we pulled into Di Franco's restaurant and had dinner. We started talking to the locals about the town. One guy was complaining that the town hadn't grown much in a hundred years, because there was no railroad or a centralized location for a freeway. This was just what we wanted to hear, and we stayed. Then a little later you and Sam came into our lives and we started living again."

"Jeff, have you ever wondered why Sam and I never had children?" She asked.

Jeff said, "I assumed, You and Sam were happy by yourselves."

"No that wasn't it. We saw the pain you two were going through and we just said we couldn't endure that kind of punishment. I suppose it was selfish of us, but that's the way we saw it," Alice explained… Jeff came over to her and gave her a hug, saying, "I'm so sorry, Alice. If I'd known, maybe I could have fought off the pain more in private." The two stared at each other, showing a genuine love for each other, before Alice changed the subject.

"All these pictures around this room have a significance to your writing?" Jeff replied, "Yes." Alice asked, "This picture of you, a black horse and a bunch of foreign cowboys, have a hidden story? I don't remember ever seeing this picture before." Her snoopiness was becoming bolder. She was right about not seeing the picture, but then she hadn't seen a lot of the newly hung pictures. Jeff was trying anything to get himself motivated for writing his new challenge. He had doubled the number of pictures to more than a hundred.

Jeff smiled with fond memories and walked up to the photograph, "Marilyn received a letter from Juan Guterrez from Argentina. You may think it's unusual to receive mail from someone you have never heard of, but with Marilyn's books all over the world, it was more common, than not. He wrote telling her that after reading most of her books about animals and how loving they were, he felt she should come and see his pony and a young calf, who would not leave each other's side. Marilyn said she had to go search out the story. I went with her for security reasons, not thinking I would be there more than a week. After a few days of boredom Juan decided to assign me a horse called Black Satin to ride with him and the gaucho's, moving cattle to different locations for grazing. Marilyn stayed with the two animals, even to the point of sleeping in their stall at night."

"Marilyn wrote two books during the time we were there. The first one was titled Heart and Soul; *Heart* for the pony and *Soul* for the calf. She swore the two were speaking to each other, so she added dialogue between them. It was hilarious. The second book was about *Me* and *Black Satin*. She described how the Gaucho's converted me from a drugstore cowboy, to an actual horseman." They lived in Argentina for six months. Jeff became an excellent rider. The Gauchos were always pulling pranks on Jeff, in good fun, and vice versa. On their last week there, the Gauchos brought in a wild horse from the pampas remote area for Jeff to break. Marilyn did not like this challenge one bit. But for Jeff, this was a must, challenge.

The rules were simple: The Gauchos would saddle the horse and it did not matter how many times Jeff got bucked off, he would have to get back on and ride it until it stopped for ten seconds with him on board. Jeff approached this challenge, like everything he did in life, with an absolute positive outcome of success. He must not fail.

Jeff rode the wild thing, getting bucked off three times, with Marilyn wanting him to abandon this foolishness each time. He gave a smile to the Gauchos who sat at the top of the make shift circled corral and showed a thumbs up of confidence. A cheer came from the fence sitters. When Jeff made good on His gesture by riding the wild thing to a standstill, the Gauchos would always remember that the American city slicker, Jeffrey Williams, rode a wild horse to a standstill.

Hey Jeff, "Let's get back to your book problem. How about I take your completed chapter's home and read them? I've read every book you've written, so I know your style. Marilyn often brought your unedited work to me to get my view."

"Oh so it was you, when she said, a friend would critique my book?" He surmised. She said, "Yes." Jeff was surprised, "I never knew that. I thought it was someone in her literary group downtown. Go ahead and take it, and maybe you can end my insanity... Something has come to mind, now that we are sharing so much of our lives. What was Marilyn apologizing for when she couldn't finish her last words to me?"

Alice asked him with trepidation, "Marilyn told me to ask you about whatever was troubling her for years. She couldn't speak much more. She started to apologize again, then she fell asleep."

Jeff knew what Marilyn was referring to, but chose to put it out of his mind, "I'll have to think about what it could have been."

CHAPTER 2

It was Saturday morning, there was just a glimmer of sunlight through the scattered clouds and the trees. This was going to be a fine morning for golf, *Josh* thought. He walked around the busted typewriter carrying a new/used replacement, shaking his head in disbelief as he looked on. As he entered with a loud knock on the back door it jarred Jeff out of the most restful sleep he'd had in months.

Passing the bedroom door, Josh, headed straight to the writing room, carrying a Black Royal Standard typewriter placing it on the desk where distinct markings of the previous machines remained, "Hey Dad, are you still in bed? Let's go play a round of golf." He'd purchased this typewriter at his school, the University of Connecticut at Storrs, where he was a graduate student in biological sciences. This was number six, and it too could suffer the same fate as the other five, if Jeff didn't give up the proven insanity of writing a book about Marilyn.

"What time is it, Son?" Yelling from the bedroom.

"It's six-thirty," Josh replied.

Jeff sounded, "My God, I haven't slept this late in years. I must have been really tired."

"Could it be; you feel better about your book?"

"Ah, gee, did Alice call you about what I did yesterday?"

Josh answered laughing, "Yes she did Dad, and she asked me to pick up another used typewriter from the school store." Josh placed the typewriter on the exact same pad marks the other departed from. He went to the window and looked out at the busted typewriter embedded in the moist lawn just inches from the sidewalk. "Good thing you didn't throw it on the sidewalk and scatter pieces everywhere, like last month. Hopefully, you can make this one last longer than a month," Josh suggested in jest.

"That piece of junk never did work well, son. If it hadn't jammed so much, maybe I'd have kept it around longer."

Josh raised his voice, "It's not the typewriter's fault, dad, it's this book you're trying to finish. Two years on a book is far too long for you. For me, that would have been a fast completion."

Jeff yelled back, "I'm going to take a quick shower." Josh sat down in his dad's chair and placed his hands on the desk alongside where the new/used typewriter now sat, and just three feet away from his mother's desk, facing him. Her electric typewriter and chair, still as untouched as before she died. Her computer sat next to the typewriter. She didn't have the same quirks as Jeff did about switching over from typewriters to computers. Josh pivoted 360 degrees in the chair, taking note of how many more pictures his dad had hung. He knew the reason for hanging more pictures; it was to stimulate his brain from the past… This was not his favorite room, for sure. Josh rolled his dad's chair backward to the bookshelf and reached for the thirty-two-page manuscript, which showed a good deal of fraying from repeated use. It had changed his life forever. The manuscript lay conspicuously, on the shelf between Jeff's twenty-seven novels and Marilyn's fourteen children's books that she'd written with such great pleasure.

Growing up, Josh wanted to be a writer like Jodie would have been, so He could please his dad and mom, but it wasn't in him. The harder he tried, the worse it affected his life. At age ten, he attended a birthday party for his best friend, Tony, down the street. After the party he called home and asked if he could stay the night. The next day Marilyn came to pick him up and found Josh was reluctant to leave with her. His eyes, giving way to tears, he asked very softly, "Could I stay here for always?" Marilyn was so surprised at his request that all she could say was… get in the car. Jeff and Marilyn were shocked and dismayed by Josh's attitude. They soon discovered that they were trying to make, Little Josh, into Jodie.

It was harder for Jeff to bring himself to understand that Josh was not going to be like their daughter. Marilyn, on-the-other-hand, quickly found herself voicing things that were relevant to the problem and adjusted well. Jeff was different. He always found that speaking his mind was not as good as writing his thoughts. They both struggled trying to find ways to show they loved him for who he was.

A few weeks later Jeff brought the thirty-two-page manuscript to the kitchen to show Marilyn,

"What's this, Jeffrey?" She looked at the title: "Our Loves for Josh and Jodie". She hesitated to take it from his hand, but then put it to her chest and sat down at the kitchen table to read it. She knew, full well, when Jeff wrote from the heart, it was always emotional. She began to read aloud, "I write today to tell you our love for the both of you." Her voice starting to quiver, she temporarily went silent, then continued to read to herself.

When she finished the last page, fighting back tears, she got up from her chair to see Jeff rummaging through the fridge looking for a left over snack.

Jeff looked over at her, "Oh, you finished it?" Not saying a thing, she went over to him, pulled him away from the fridge, closed the door, and wrapped her arms around him.

"Just hold me and say nothing… you've written words that make me feel wonderful. These words will really help Josh… and me," Marilyn's voice was down to a whisper.

Jeff took the manuscript from her hands and put it on the counter, and opened it, saying, "How about signing it; 'With Love, Mom and Dad'. Your handwriting is so much better than mine." Josh was changed after reading his dad's family story... as were Marilyn and Jeff.

Jeff finished his shower, dressed, and was already heading to the back door with his clubs, when he yelled, "C'mon son, I thought you were in a hurry!" Josh looked over at his mother's picture on the desk and gestured a kiss, "We love you mom." Quickly placing the manuscript back on the shelf between his mother's and dad's books, he ran out the back, whisked past the typewriter, then sprinted to his car. His dad was already sitting on the passenger side as if to say c'mon son, I'm waiting on you!

Josh slid into the driver's seat of his Volkswagen bus and fastened his seat belt, which was a "must do" for the family. "Well son, what time do we tee off?" Josh said, "I didn't make reservations at the club."

"What? So you actually think we can just walk into the club and pick our own starting time?" Jeff queried.

"Well, I was thinking, we'd go pickup *Joe Al* at his barber salon and then find *Mr. Mitchell*, who I'm sure does not work at psychiatry on weekends; and you, a world renowned author should make it happen. Between the three of you, how would they not let us play." Jeff just shook his head with a grin. Josh gave his mothers' smile and pulled out of the driveway.

Josh, drove over to the barber salon, following all the rules of a good driver, knowing full well that his dad was eyeing his every move. You do not throw caution and speed to the wind when Jeffrey Williams is in the car.

Josh pulled up to the salon. Jeff rolled down the window and yelled, "Hey Spinga, let's go play a round of golf." Joe Al didn't have to look through the shop windows to know who was calling. Joe Al got the nickname, Spinga one night when he, Jeff and Mark Mitchell were at a fish fry up in New Brunswick. The three had sat down at the table and soon the Portuguese waiter brought three plates loaded with cod, a pile of potatoes and a hefty salad. Joe Al was busy talking about where the three were from, to other diners, as the waiter warned them the fish had bones. Joe Al, not hearing a word, dug in. His second bite was all it took. He started choking when a guy yelled, "He has a spinga stuck in his throat" … Meaning a fish bone, and that nickname never left him.

Joe Al, holding up his finger at the door to indicate, one minute, turned to his employees and issued orders to handle the clientele while he was away. A few moaned at his leaving, because Saturday's are the busiest day of the week. It didn't matter to him, though, golfing with his friends was far more important.

Spinga jumped into the back seat of the Volks Bus and immediately quipped, "So you threw another typewriter out the window, huh?" Jeff looked at Josh, "Word spreads fast around here, apparently."

Josh quickly looked forward, "Don't look at me dad, I didn't say anything."

Josh drove a few blocks and into the driveway of Mark Mitchell. Mark was sitting on an old elm stump, waiting for his ride. When Josh stopped next to Mark, Jeff leaned over and yelled, "I take it, you knew we were coming?"

"Yes, a little birdie told me," Mark said cheerfully.

"I'll bet it was a female birdie who lives next door to me," Jeff remarked as Mark jumped onto the back seat with Spinga, ignoring Jeff's comment.

Mark declared, "I have a bone to pick with you, Jeff." Not waiting for Jeff to ask what it was, he proceeded. "You couldn't ask for my help in ironing out your problems. I'm a psychiatrist, for heaven sake, why didn't you ask for my help?"

"I have," Jeff responded firmly. "Over and over, and all I got from you was; 'I haven't a clue why you throw typewriters out the window.'" They all started laughing at the comedy of Jeff's behavior. A long time before, Alice had picked the Hollywood characters of Abbott & Costello to best describe the two in the back seat. Sam asked who was who? Alice had smiled, 'It doesn't matter.'

When they arrived at the club, a foursome was waiting their turn to tee off. It didn't look good for them. Spinga volunteered to go and ask for permission to jump to the head of the line. When he returned, he smiled, "Let's play golf." The three were anxious to ask how he did it, but they remained mum, not wanting to tick off the other foursomes… especially now that two groups were ready to start, and they were jumping ahead.

"Okay, guys," announced Spinga, as he pulled out his scorecard. "Who's going to break sixty today? Come on, we can do this. Is Josh going to be the only one that ever goes below sixty?" Jeff looked over at Mark who was ready to address the ball, "The answer is yes," replied Jeff.

Spinga shook his head in disgust, "Okay let's go play 9 holes."

After nearly two hours, and creating a foursome backlog, the group was finishing the ninth hole. Josh was ready to putt when suddenly Mark asked the curious question, "How'd you get us ahead of the pack when they had reservations and we didn't?" All three stood waiting for an expensive answer.

"It was simple," replied Spinga, "I told the manager that I would have my Candy, in my shop, give him a full body massage, on the house." They all had seen Candy and agreed that was a great deal for the manager. When they finished marking their totals for the nine holes, Jeff anxiously asked, "So who finished under sixty? I have sixty-three."

Mark smiled, "I beat you by one, Jeff."

"I have forty-seven," declared Josh, which everyone knew was going to be the best score. But when Spinga, proudly announced his score of fifty-one, the three looked at each other, and without hesitation, blew off Spinga, as cheating. The three started for the car.

"Hey, wait a minute, I could've had that score, but you guys talked too much while I was putting, so I think I deserve a fifty-one."

When they piled into the car, Jeff sighed, "Now I'm ready to get back to my book." They looked at each other as if to say, that's not a good idea.

"Okay. So you guys think I should forget about the book, huh?" Jeff asked.

"Why put yourself through all this when you don't have to," suggested Mark.

"Because I've never had this problem with any of my books, and I must complete this last one," Jeff insisted. They all looked at each other again, hearing the words, 'Last book.' Okay, okay, you're all looking at me like I'm going to commit suicide, or something. Well, I wouldn't murder myself." Spinga grabbed his arm, "You wouldn't commit murder of your friends, would you?

"Spinga, I wouldn't commit murder of you guys, my neighbors, myself, or anyone in this world, so just stop this crazy conversation and let's go home," Josh started the van.

CHAPTER 3

Snowflakes began to fall outside Jake's Roadside Café, making this the earliest measureable snowfall in years, and giving locals an excuse to bet on the amount of snowfall before Christmas. Jeff, on his morning jog, and nearing the halfway point of two miles, stopped and went in to learn the latest about the weather. He'd hear a lot more than just the weather. These regulars live to tell stories of the past and gossip literally about everybody and everything.

Jeff said hi to everyone, then went to the counter. The main topic for today was whether the weather will be good for the Jazz Festival in two weeks, or bad. The consensus in the diner, it would be bad. Elaine, the waitress, had already put his glass of water in front of him as he laid a dollar bill next to it. Jeff had always felt it was a good trade off, one dollar for one glass of water. Yes, this meant not wearing a bottle strapped to him and fighting the jiggling, half-empty container all the way home. Elaine, for years, had argued with him about the dollar, but she finally relinquished and just accepted it with a smile and a thank you. He quickly downed the water.

As Jeff got near the door Homer yelled from across the room, "Hey Jeffrey, am I in your next book?" "Homer, I already put you in book four. Now if you go out and bungee jump off some bridge, maybe I'll slip you in the next one."

"Well then Jeffrey, it's safe to say I won't be in your next book," kidded Homer. Jeff laughed as he left the café. Nearing Alice's house, and slowing down to a walk, he saw her opening the garage door, then backing out her new BMW. When he got near her window, she powered her window down. He was hoping she had some news about why he was stymied on the book. "Good morning, Jeff."

"And good morning to you, Alice, with a shortness of breath. You're off to the office, are you?" "Yes, Jeff, like every early morning it's off to work, work, work. If I don't set the example, then my agents won't work at selling homes, either"

"Are you ready for the Jazz Festival?"

"Yes."

"The guys at the diner feel it's going to be an early winter."

"That means we'll have a late winter… I'm sorry I have to rush off, Jeff, but I really have to get to work." "Oh sure… don't let me hold you up."

When she started to drive off, she looked in the rearview mirror and saw him staring at her car. She stopped and backed up, "Jeff, about your book, I've called a friend of mine. She's a psychologist, Joan Steele. Hopefully she can help me, because I am at a loss." Jeff stood silent as Alice waved goodbye and drove down the street. All he could think of was that now two shrinks will be working on his problem and they'll both come up with nothing.

Jeff went into his home and did exactly the predictable thing. He filled a bowl with cereal, added milk, then peeled a banana, and went to his desk to eat and write. His stymied period of writing had caused him a vast emptiness. He leaned back in his chair after finishing the cereal and began thinking about what his golfing buddies had said: "Don't you get so depressed, that you murder yourself." He kept telling himself that something must change, because if it didn't, he could fall into a pit of despair, resulting in tragedy.

He put two papers in his typewriter so it would be ready to go when a flash of genius swept his brain, but after an hour none came. What did come was a need to sleep, a typical condition for depression and anxiety.

After several minutes of fighting drowsiness, he pushed the typewriter back, laid his head down on his arms and fell into a deep sleep. He began to dream about Marilyn. It was a fun dream. *Jodie was in the writing room editing her dad's new book, at least thinking she was helping. Josh was there too, nudging Jodie to pick him up from his stroller. Marilyn was taking notes of the children's actions for her next book. Jeff had a big grin on his face as he slept. At times nearly laughing aloud. The phone began to ring, so Marilyn got up to answer it.* Suddenly, Jeff awoke to the blare of a smoke alarm detector. Catching reality, he sat up, rubbed his eyes and realized the phone was ringing.

He reached for it near the edge of the desk. "Hello?" Sounding foggy headed, he yawned.

"Hi Jeff, this is the girls across the street, *Jamie* and *Carly*."

"Oh, hi," still sounding groggy.

"Can we come over for dinner? We'll pick up some food at Jay's Pizza and bring it over about six. If that's okay with you?"

"Oh I get it. You want to console me, and talk me out of it."

Carly shrugged her shoulders in jest to Jamie. "Sort of, I guess."

"Sure you can come over tonight. But since when do you have to ask, when to come over?"

It felt good to hear the girl's voices. They'd been on vacation for two weeks and Jeff had missed them. "The girls," as Jeff liked to call them, were his and Marilyn's favorite couple on the block after Sam and Alice; they liked playing cards and dominoes. In the past, the four of them often played into the late hours of night.

When he put the phone down, he had the urge to write. The paper was already in the typewriter so he took advantage of the urge. It may be the exactly what I need to begin writing like before… He started to write: *The girls are coming over tonight to challenge Marilyn and I, to a game of wit. We're going to show those two who controls the table. I, I, think…* his mind went blank. It was like a power surge shot through the light bulb, and it blew it out. As sudden as he had the urge to write, the feeling disappeared.

He stood up, grabbed the base of the typewriter, lifted it for a second, then re-settled his emotions along with the typewriter.

He sat back down in his writing chair, hoping to return to his dream. It didn't return. The rest of the day left him with such disappointment that he decided to call the girls and cancel. Reaching for the phone, the doorbell rang. He looked at the vintage clock behind Marilyn's desk and realized it was six o'clock, and they were already there.

He opened the front door to the smiles of the two friends and invited them in. They could see he had just woken up with messed hair and swollen eyes and was not ready for company. Jamie was still holding the food from Jay's when she asked, "You forgot that we were coming over? Maybe we should go?"

"Please don't. I'm just down these days and maybe I can absorb some of your cheery attitude."

Carly nudged Jamie to put the food down on the table. The two quickly organized the room making it immediately more presentable and pleasing; and they all sat to enjoy Jay's take-out. When they finished eating Jamie cleared the table and the two did the dishes. Jeff had already retrieved the cards and score paper for the anticipated game. He shuffled the cards, waiting for them to finish, until he got tired of waiting. "Hey Girls, forget that stuff, I'll do them in the morning."

The girls looked at each other and back at Jeff. Carly spoke first. "We're not here to play cards, Jeff."

"Oh I'm sorry, I'll get the dominoes," he said amiably. Jamie, responded nervously, "No we didn't come to play games."

"I know. You came over to get me out of my depression. Alice is recruiting everyone to help solve my problems, but I must work this out myself."

Carly cautiously struggled to find the right words without stuttering. They began speaking at the same time when Jeff demanded to know what they were hesitant about. Suddenly Jamie blurted the words, "We want your semen."

The voices all fell silent… Jeff swallowed hard, to keep from spewing his food everywhere, "You want, what from me?"

Both began to speak, with the chatter of an auctioneer. "Stop, both of you. I can't do that! It would break my trust with Marilyn."

"I think Marilyn would say yes to our request," Carly said boldly.

"You say that because you want your way with this."

Carly jumped in, "You wrote about this in your book *Lives and Meanings* to *Each Other*, and that gave us the idea."

"Carly, please, it was just a fictional novel, not real life," Jeff flatly stated.

Jamie chimed in, "Carly and I feel that our biological clocks are ticking into oblivion and it is time to make this happen."

"Jamie, everyone's clock is going terminal," Jeff insisted this was not proper.

Carly, nearing tears, began to explain, "We went on vacation the last two weeks to adopt a baby. It was the same thing wherever we went, they want a father and a mother, not two of the same sex. We have been working to adopt, for a year."

"I'm sorry girls, but my conscience will not allow me do this. I'm sure there are plenty of guys who will welcome selling their semen. The word even seems smirky and trashy."

Jamie lowered her head, "We know you, and if the two of us ever knew a man, it would be you."

Carly got up from the table and Jamie followed, "We are very sorry to have inconvenienced you."

"Now listen you two, this better not change how we feel about each other. So give me a hug and let me pay for our meal."

When the three got to the door, Jamie turned to Jeff and lamented, "It would have been such a wonderful child." Jeff smiled, and gave them both a peck on the cheek, closing the door behind them. He went to the writing room and sat down to his typewriter with a smile. He looked across the desk at Marilyn's typewriter and her chair. "So what do you think of the girls, Marilyn? Can you believe those two? They sound like they are determined to find a sperm bank and carry out their plan." Jeff put his fingers on the type keys and thought for a moment. This may be a fun short story to write. So he began with his title *A Woman's Hunt for Sperm*. He looked up at Marilyn. "Do you like the title? Of course you do, it's your type of comedy." Seemingly, it felt like he had just sat down to begin his story, when he looked up to see the morning sun was casting light through the front window. "My God, I've been writing all night. He felt the thickness of the typed papers and yelled, "My mind is not wasted, I'm cured."

Hopping into the shower and taking it as hot as he could stand it gave him the energy to begin writing again. Every sentence he wrote gave him a need to write the next. At times he would laugh out loud at the muscle bound character that Jamie was interviewing, and the type of questions she was asking. Carly kept telling her to stop and call in another donor, because this one was too big. "Can you imagine having his child?" Carly asked. "It would probably weigh as much as you do, at birth. So interview some smaller guy. Someone who doesn't have a neck bigger than your chest." His typing seemed to drone on endlessly in thought, until finally his head bobbled and dropped onto the keys.

A knock on the window drew Jeff's attention there… "Hi Jeff, have you been writing all day?

"What day is this?" Alice frowned and didn't answer his question.

"How about coming over in half hour and have some dinner. I have someone that you should meet." "Okay, but I'm going to take a shower first."

She smiled, "Yeah, maybe you better. You have imbedded key marks on your face. Maybe with a lot of hot water, they'll disappear."

"What?" Jeff asked.

"Never mind. We'll be waiting for you." Jeff closed the window, then went to the mirror on the wall. "My goodness, I do have key marks on my chin and my eyes, looks as though they may start bleeding any moment." He sat down to call Alice and take a rain check, when he noticed how large the stack of manuscript papers had grown. He was flabbergasted at the number of pages he wrote in one night and a day. He read the last page to see if the story was complete. It was, and with that, he thanked God for the peace of mind.

Quickly, he showered, dressed and headed to Alice's back door. When Alice answered, he lunged forward and gave Alice a big hug, laughing near hysterically. "Alice, I've solved my writer's block. I wrote one-hundred twenty-six pages since yesterday." She disregarded his exuberance. "Come into the living room. I want you to meet someone." As they walked, Jeff could see she was not listening.

"Alice, I really did write half a book since yesterday. In fact, I even have a title, *A Woman's Hunt for Sperm.* She stuck out her hand stopping Jeff from taking another step, but it was too late, her guest overheard the title. Rolling her eyes, Alice introduced the two. *Joan*, this is my neighbor and friend Jeffrey Williams. Jeff, this is *Joan Steele.* She's a Clinical Psychologist over at Hartford. She does a T.V. show in New York, that deals with psychology.

"She's looking for a home, possibly to buy in this area. She'll be staying here until after the Jazz Festival on Sunday." The three sat down to dinner. Alice and Joan made small talk while Jeff just smiled occasionally as he ate. When the three finished eating and cleared the table, Jeff removed himself to his favorite living room chair, ready to talk about his new writings. Alice and Joan sat on the couch still making small talk about the types of homes in the area. Jeff got right to the subject he wanted to talk about. "Oh, by the way Alice, why do you always think a shrink can solve my problems."

"I don't know Jeff, but I want to help you anyway I can, and it seems the best approach is the way your brain works. Don't you agree?" Jeff evaded the question and began his own questions to Ms. Steele

"So, Joan, what is your expertise in psychology?"

"Sexual compatibility in marriage," Joan fired back.

Jeff's mind began rolling with questions, "Do you have children?"

"Yes, two, a boy and a girl. Roxanne is twenty-four, and Robert is twenty-two. They both live in Hong Kong and work in finance. I don't get to see them as much as I'd like."

"Does your husband find it wonderful to have a wife that is so compatible?"

Alice was getting irritated with Jeff's line of questioning, "I think you're asking Joan, far too many personal questions... it sounds more like an inquisition than cordial conversation."

"It's all right Alice, I'll answer that. I'm divorced. In fact, I've been divorced four times and will never marry again." Alice became red faced because of how Jeff was acting. She grabbed his arm and lead him to the door. Joan quickly added, "No, no, Alice, it's refreshing to hear a man actually say what he is thinking."

"Well, if I was out of line, I'm very sorry. I haven't slept for two days and I'm a bit addled. It's just that I have found my cure for writer's block and now I'm ready to go to sleep," Jeff apologized.

"I would really love to read *A Woman's Hunt for Sperm,* if I may. With a title like that, it stirs my appetite," she grinned.

"Sure, anytime. I like your choice of words Ms. Steele, they go well with my title," Jeff was awake now.

Jeff looked at Alice, then at Joan, "How about right now?" I'll have it in your hands in one minute and twenty seconds."

He was out of the house in a flash and back in less than his predicted time. Handing Joan the manuscript and taking deep breaths to fill his lungs, he smiled, "Keep it as long as you want."

She said, "That won't be necessary, I'll read it right now." Jeff chuckled, "that's what my wife would say." He lowered his head, "I'm sorry, I'm way past tired. I think I'll catch a few winks while you read."

Joan sat on the couch and began to read. As she finished each page, Alice picked them up and read, also. Jeff slid back in the recliner and in short order was fast asleep. Even with Joan breaking into an uncontrollable laughter, it didn't faze his sleep. Alice was also laughing, but she was seeing something that resembled the girls across the street.

When the two finished reading, they commented back and forth about how clever Jeff's approach was with both a humorous and a serious side to the characters. Joan looked at him, then turned to Alice, "He is truly a gifted writer."

"His books have sold all over the world, Joan, and he has tons of literary awards, which he takes no pleasure in receiving. He still feels unsatisfied. Even when Marilyn was alive, he was not content with his work."

Alice got up from the couch and pulled a heavy blanket from her cedar chest and draped it over Jeff, tucking it around his neck, and sat down again. "Now that you've met Jeff and read some of his writing style, have you come up with any conclusions?"

"You probably should have told him that my main reason was to help him, and not so much look for a home just yet."

"Believe me Joan, Jeff knows in his heart that we are trying to help him and he appreciates our doing so. But, his mind is so entrenched in writing this book about Marilyn, that we are hopelessly handicapped at bringing him out of the doldrums."

"Could we go into the kitchen and talk? I'm afraid he's going to wake. I have something to tell you about how I do therapy," Joan said in a whisper.

"Sure." Alice put Jeff's new story, all one hundred twenty-six pages, on the coffee table, then the two went to the kitchen. Before sitting down, Joan declared, "I can't help Jeff." Alice was shocked at such a quick decision.

The two sat down at the table and Joan reached for Alice's hand and clinched. "You see what I'm doing, Alice?"

"You're holding my hand for reasons that I don't understand."

"This is what I do in my one-on-one therapy class. I touch, if need be, I hug. The reasoning behind this is that a marriage becomes less and less touching, day by day. Eventually the zip disappears and the couple looks outside their marriage. This is why I reinvent the touch and holding procedure. If I'm successful, the couple will return to the lust they had for each other, when they first married. With Jeff I have nothing to bring him back to. He has written a book, or he has written half a book and now he wants to finish it without Marilyn when it's all about her. He writes a hundred twenty-six pages of a good comical plot and thinks his writing problems are solved, when they're not. It's far different than writing about his wife."

"Why can't you just show him that he has a lot of love to give to someone else?" Alice asked.

"Alright, you've got it, Alice. I'll work with you two and I'll guarantee that the two of you, as long as you try, will make a loving couple in the next six months."

"That sounds crazy. Jeff and I are best friends. Besides, I would be breaking Marilyn's trust in me… If I may ask, why did your four marriages fail?"

"Hummm… You criticized Jeff for getting personal, and now you're doing it, but that's okay. I want to explain… My first husband discovered he liked men more, and the more I touched him the worse it became. The second husband was a polygamist. He went to jail. So, maybe you can understand why I should have stopped there. My third was a producer for my television program. He was sleeping with my assistant, and my fourth wanted to live off my income and travel all over the world. He was the father of my children."

Alice became apologetic, "I am so sorry, I asked."

"Sometimes it's better to rehash these things, so I don't forget and make the same mistakes over again," Joan lamented.

"I have an idea, Joan. After I leave for the office tomorrow morning, maybe you can go to Jeff's with some sandwiches and have lunch. In the meantime, I'll keep looking for a home for you to buy, and who knows, maybe you're more ready to buy than you realize."

"You persist that I work with Jeff, so I'll give it a try… Are you going to leave Jeff sleeping in that recliner all night?"

"He never sleeps more than a couple hours at a stretch. He'll wake up and go home."

"If you want to stay up longer, Joan, go right ahead. It'll get cold during the night, so just grab that quilt that's on the foot locker and drape it over the bed spread."

Joan gave Alice a hug, "It's eleven o'clock. Time for me to turn in, also. I have one more thing to say, about Jeff. He has not solved his writing problems. He was suddenly energized by something that loosed him to write those hundred and twenty-six pages. If he could mentally channel that same quickening to the book about Marilyn then I would say his problems might possibly be solved, but I think it involves something far deeper.

CHAPTER 4

It was beginning to snow slightly when Jeff bolted from the back door at six a.m. for his morning run. He stopped at his front gate to stretch and get his leg muscles limbered. He looked down the street to see if the girls were planning to jog with him, but nothing was stirring at their house. Feeling charged from solving his writer's block, he ran the two miles in his best time in two years, in spite of the bad weather.

Alice was walking to her detached garage when Jeff waved and hollered as he came from down the street. "Good morning, Alice."

"You sound awfully chipper this morning, Jeff."

"I feel so good. It's like my life, all of a sudden, became simple."

"By the way, Jeff, Joan will bring over lunch for you."

"Why? I don't need food. I have plenty. Besides, I'm anxious to continue Marilyn's book."

"She just wants to be with somebody while I'm at work."

"I'm not a baby sitter, and I'm betting you're setting me up for a shrink session."

"Be nice, Jeff, and just maybe you'll learn something from her. She is very smart. Now, good-by." Jeff was trying to muster enough snow to make a snowball to throw at her, but she drove out to fast.

Jeff went to his front door, rather than chance Joan seeing him walking around back and maybe wanting to come over now. He went straight to the writing room and put paper in the typewriter. Then he settled into his chair, ready to begin. He sat for a moment clearing his mind about lunch and having to entertain "Joan the intruder."

There he sat waiting for some figment of thought to enter his brain and extend to his fingers tips, so he could begin the second half of Marilyn's book. Like before, nothing was coming through. Jeff was nearly ready to make another typewriter exit the room, when he heard foot sounds coming from the back decking of Alice's home. His curiosity got the better of him as he rolled his chair back to the window. He squinted for a second, then realized it was Joan exercising on the decking.

He stared at her, noticing how different she looked compared to the night before. Her workout outfit molded to her body as though she was naked, leaving little to the imagination.

With a sigh, he murmured, 'dressing like that probably created some of the problems in her life.' He closed the blinds and put his mind back on course.

For the next two hours, he went through mental anguish waiting for something to grow in his brain that would give him his starting sentence, and then have the same results of yesterday's writing of *A Woman's Hunt for Sperm* gave him.

He stared out the front window watching an occasional car pass down the street. He knew most of the people driving past, but still wondered where they were going. They must have a much simpler life than he did. He reasoned, talking aloud, 'Some will be going to work and other's will be off; probably going shopping with their spouses, or maybe just going for a drive to get out of the house. Whatever they're doing, they'll be together for the evening meal.'

A knock on the back door broke Jeff's train of thought. He glanced at the clock. "Ah, crap, its noon. It must be, 'Joan the Intruder.'" He took his time answer the door, hoping she might become impatient and leave. When he opened the door, she smiled, "Were you hoping I would have left before you opened the door?"

"Of course not Joan, I was looking forward to having lunch with you."

"You're a good liar, Jeff, but I want to help you, so bear with me. I made lasagna." His eyebrows raised knowing that's his favorite food. He pointed to the kitchen and she led the way. He resigned himself to the fact that a half hour lunch would not be that hard to endure. After all, a person has to eat, he thought.

He politely asked her what she wanted to drink. She responded, "Oh, anything."

He reached up in the top shelf of the cabinet above the sink and pulled out a bottle of scotch and placed it in front of her plate. She looked at him with a smile, "Don't you have a glass?" Jeff frowned, then smiled, "I like your sense of humor. I'll get you a soda." She stopped him. "I'll have a drink if you have one."

"I don't normally have hard liquor before five. In fact, I haven't had a drink since the last jazz festival. But if you want a drink, I'll have one with you." Joan was trying to figure this guy out and if it took a drink to loosen him up, she was willing to give it a test. Jeff put some water in his drink and looked at Joan to see if she wanted some water. She nodded with an affirmative. Then he reached for some ice in the freezer and looked at her. Again, a nod, yes.

The two were on their third drink without giving the lasagna a second glance. She knew that her body had a higher tolerance for alcohol than most men. After all it was at the Missouri

Compromise Bar in Missouri, that she met her second husband. He was a look-alike for Tom Selleck, so drunk or otherwise, she knew the guy was the one for her. They were married just hours later. The next week he went to jail for polygamy.

The three drinks wouldn't defuse her brain, even though this approach was as unorthodox as you can get for a trained and highly respected psychologist. Joan remained resolute and determined to find out Jeff's problem even if it took getting him inebriated.

After the fourth drink Joan explained to Jeff how she handled clients and why she was so successful: "Jeff, I'm going to hold your hand."

"So what's so big about that?"

"It's not that big a deal, but that's only step one."

"Oh."

"Now we're just going to hold hands across the table like this for as long as you want." It sounded foolish at first, but then his mind began to go back to when Marilyn was in this very kitchen and the two of them held each other often. She knew, she was treading in dangerous territory, when he squeezed her hand. Something was going on in his brain and Joan was waiting for his next reaction.

Jeff pulled his hands away, leaving Joan to begin withdraw hers. "I need another drink before I answer any more of your questions."

"Maybe, Jeff, you shouldn't have another." Jeff was already pouring and then put some ice cubes and handed Joan, hers. They both began to drink. Joan, for the first time in her illustrious career, didn't know where this was heading. Because of Jeff's mild manner, she let it play out.

When they both emptied their glasses, Jeff asked a simple question, "Have you ever acted in a play?"

"A few"

"Can I ask you to star in my play."

"I don't follow you. To be perfectly honest with you, Jeff, I feel like you're the psychologist here and I'm the subject."

"I know better, Joan, you're very good at what you do and that's why I'm going to ask you this question: "Would you play Marilyn for me? Sit with me on the couch."

"You want me to lay on the couch with you and do it?"

"No, no, no, I want you to sit with me and tell me, from Marilyn's point of view, why I can't finish this book."

"I read your half book about Marilyn early this morning… It could be just writers block and nothing else."

"Do you really believe that?"

"No."

"I don't either. So, here's what I'm asking you… Maybe we can have another drink, then you and I can sit on the couch, we can hold each other and talk about the book."

"I don't need another drink to do that, but I don't like the way this is going." He shrugged her off, guiding her to the couch. Her sweaty palms were telling her to put a stop to this experiment gone bad, when Jeff asked, "Marilyn, how was your day?"

Joan responded, "Well Jeffrey, I wrote my first book today. So, I deserve a kiss for that." Joan was shocked her words came out that way, and wanted to take them back. Before she could correct her words Jeff came closer and kissed her on the cheek. "Huh, it seems the reward doesn't match the achievement." Again she was sorry for her words gesturing it was the booze. They both laughed and continued the play until Jeff went to the writing room and brought back the book on Marilyn. "Have you given this book a title?" She asks hoping to bring him back to reality.

"Not yet."

"If I were giving it a title," she declared, "it would be, *Forever Yours, Jeff.*"

"Let's continue our play." This is not what Joan wanted to do. Jeff was enjoying this, almost non-fiction play. The two laughed and at times cried, but were truly living another life they both brought to the scene.

The phone rang at 6 o'clock and they both sprang from the couch with guilt written all over their faces. Jeff answered the phone with a slight quiver. "Hello… Hi Alice." Jeff listened. "Yes, Joan is here."

"Tell Alice, I'm heading home right now." When Jeff hung up he acknowledged that Alice asked him to come for dinner, too. "I'm not going," he tells Joan, "I want to digest everything we did today." He leans in and gives Joan a big hug and a kiss on the cheek. "Are we still doing the 'play'?"

"No. I really appreciate what you did for me."

"Well, we didn't touch the lasagna, so you have plenty to eat." Jeff walked her to the door, then he went hurriedly to the study. He threw a paper in the typewriter and began at the center of the page, *Forever Yours, Jeff.* With a smile he sat back in the chair and looked at the title, then remarked, 'Thanks Joan you may have broken my writer's block.'

Joan entered Alice's back door, to find Alice standing there in disbelief. "You've been over at Jeff's for six hours?" Joan, still intoxicated, tried to speak normally, but the liquor was slurring her speech. "Are you drunk?"

Alice, you told me to help Jeff come out of his emotional quagmire, so I decided to weaken his psyche a bit."

"By getting him drunk? Is that how you treat all your clientele?"

"Of course not. In fact, I've never done that before, but his brilliance is so far above anyone I've ever known, that I let him choose the method in which to open up to me."

"Do you think you helped him?"

"I think it was a first step." Joan chose not to tell Alice about the "play" part, fearing the reaction she may get. "Maybe I should go over tomorrow, at noon, and work with him some more."

"You make it sound like you're intrigued by him."

"Alice are you jealous that I'm trying to help Jeffrey?"

"I'm just looking out for Jeff's best interest." Alice was no fool, she could see something that told her Joan was impressed by her neighbor and best friend.

The next morning, Alice pulled out of her driveway and looked down the street for her jogging friend, but he was nowhere to be seen. She hesitated for a minute, then drove back in the driveway. There, she caught a glimpse of Jeff in his study, typing. With a smile on her face, she left home feeling good that maybe Joan's methods were justified.

Jeff could hear Karen Sawyer's barking dog down the street. He opened the blinds a little more and could see the taillights of Alice's car moving down the street. He craned his neck around to see if Joan was on the patio. He told himself, 'Come on Jeff, get back to solving your problem.' He gave a second look at the patio, then turned back to reviewing his notes that summarized the meeting between him and Joan.

At exactly ten o'clock, Joan came out to the patio for her morning workout. It was a beautiful, fifty-five-degree morning with the sun warming the air. She turned on her portable radio, keeping it low, so not to disturb the neighbors and began her stretches and twists. Some might call it low-impact workout, but it impacted Jeff more than Joan.

He walked to the window and raised the blinds. They both saw each other. He was hesitant, then opened the window, "Good morning Jeff." "Good morning to you Joan."

"You want me to bring over roast beef sandwiches at noon?"

"If you like."

"I like."

"Is this more therapy?" She laughed without answering and went back to her workout.

Right at twelve, Joan knocked at Jeff's back door. "Nobody can say you're not prompt."

"I've always been that way… so are you ready for lunch? You seemed to have answered the door a lot quicker than yesterday." Jeff didn't respond. He noticed that she had a backpack. "Are you planning to eat out…? I was thinking that you could sit in Marilyn's chair in the study and I would sit at mine. Then maybe, we can toss around ideas of how the two of us worked face to face."

"No Jeff, it was fine to do the 'play' idea once, but it's not healthy to repeat that approach."

"Oh, I really enjoyed that, yesterday. It brought back a lot of memories."

"Yes, but you have to remember that we were both liquored up. That does not create a good case study. So if you like, I'll sit with you in this kitchen and eat or we can go somewhere to eat."

"You sound like you have some other place in mind, do you?"

"I thought we could walk down to that little stream in the park and have lunch at one of the tables. I brought a note pad, I have soda's, sandwiches, potato chips, and a pie."

"That sounds okay. I'll just slip into my jogging shoes and be ready." Joan could tell by Jeff's voice that the park wouldn't have been his first choice, but she was determined to get Jeff's problem solved in more of professional method.

The two left his house with Jeff taking the backpack from Joan and putting it on his back as they walked. "I'll give you a tour of the neighborhood as we walk."

"Well, thank you sir."

"You're very welcome ma'am." Jeff pointed, first, to the two story across the street. "This house belongs to Karen Sawyer. She models larger women's clothing. Presently, she is single."

"Alice told me about a few of these women who live here on the block."

They continued down a cobblestone path until they reached the girls house. "This is the house of my good friends. I trust them with everything I have."

"I love the house. It reminds me of a large New England cottage," Joan remarked.

Jeff went on, "Inside, it's loaded with antique furniture. You'll meet them at Alice's house party before going to the Jazz Festival. Everyone on the block will be there." Jeff began to address the house next to the girls, when he thought for a moment and says, "Not every woman on the block is single or divorced, you know, but this house belongs to Sara Labelle and she's divorced." They both laughed about his last comment. "Her ex-husband, an Army Captain, left her for a German lady, while stationed in Augsburg, Germany."

A car door slammed and Jeff turned around to see who it was. It was the girls leaving. Jeff waved, but they didn't acknowledge. So he just went on describing the other not so familiar types at the end of the block.

When they got to the park, Jeff took the backpack off and the two sat across from each other at a park table and began to eat. Joan was noticeably eager to start the discussion now that there was to be a different approach than the day before. Jeff smiled as she threw the paper plates in the trash barrel hurriedly, and sat across Jeff signaling for his hands to grasp hers.

He put his palms on hers and grinned. "What's so funny?" She asked.

"Oh it's really not important," Jeff gave off a sinister grin.

"Yes, it's very important that you be totally truthful to me." Jeff shrugged his shoulders and explained. "You're holding my hands and because of that, I am picking up vibes that tell me a whole story about you." She quickly pulled her hands back, feeling almost violated. "Please explain, Jeff, because every time I try one of my methodologies on you, it back fires."

"Well, when I was a kid, I would get these odd feelings when shaking hands with people. As I grew older it became even more pronounced. When I met Marilyn at a workshop seminar on the campus of Rutgers U… when she asked me to hold her hand and I did, we had a connection of sorts."

"So if you held my hand, you'd know if you had a special feeling for me?"

"No, it would just tell me general ideas about what and who you are to me. Let me try to give an example: Do you know what a teletype machine is?"

"No."

"Well, a teletype changes electrical impulses to a mechanical transmission, and that ends up as typed words on paper. It does it by an electrical field. When I hold someone's hand or hands I get that type of impulse. My mind fixes on the impulse and almost instantly I get a reading."

"That sounds pretty wild."

"Well I'm just warning you that when we hold hands I'm getting impulses."

"Why is it, Jeff, when I'm away from you, I'm confident that I will be in charge at our next session, then when we meet, I lose my position?" She reaches for his hands and grabs tight.

Nothing is said for a minute, then Jeff begins to smile. "Now what are you smiling about?" Joan noticed that Jeff's smile was very appealing. It was genuine and conducive, which made Joan unconformable.

"You're showing warmth and it feels like your emotions are taking hold."

"That's it Jeffrey, I can't get through to you, let's go." Not a word was said on the walk back.

CHAPTER 5

It seems that only this morning the people at the coffee shop were discussing how the weather would be for the Jazz Festival two weeks hence, and it's already here and now. Jeff was dressed, with gray slacks, white shirt, tie, and a pull over cardigan sweater, standing in the doorway of his study, reluctant to even think of partying. From nowhere, Jeff's mind flashed a need to write. Jeff quickly sat at his typewriter and began to type: My life has changed like yours did years ago…Then, as fast as the words formed on the typewriter, the follow through thoughts ended. Alice's party noise was overriding his concentration. His ability to drown out distractions was far less than he had ever known in the past, but he stubbornly remained, at the typewriter, waiting for more thoughts to form from those opening words, with hopes that his old self will take control. Suddenly, the phone rang, stunning Jeff momentarily, then he realized it was probably Alice calling for him to get his butt over there. He got up from the chair. "Yes, I'm coming, damn-it." His frustration was obvious on the phone.

"Hi dad, it sounds like maybe I shouldn't have called."

"Oh, hi Josh. I'm sorry, I thought it was Alice calling to hurry me up and come to her stupid party before the Jazz Festival… What's up?"

"It sounded like you were ready to throw another machine out the window. How would you like to go with me to Bridgeport and have lunch, tomorrow? I'd like you to meet a special woman in my life."

"Oh sure. I'd like to meet her."

"You know dad, I'm trying to find what you and mom had. Maybe she's the one…it is so difficult to find nice and good girls in the same person."

"Okay son. What time?"

"I thought, about ten o'clock, I'll pick you up. We'd get there at eleven, pick up *Cheryl*, then go to church, and afterward have lunch."

"Church?"

"Yes, Dad. You know how mom felt about attending mass every Sunday."

"Okay, son, I'll be ready," Since Marilyn's death, Jeff had not attended mass.

"…And, dad don't wear a tie! Just because mom liked to see you in ties, doesn't mean you have to wear one every time you go somewhere. I'm betting you have a tie on, right now, for the Jazz Festival." Jeff said his goodbyes with a smile and hung up. He was placing his chair to sit again, when a shout from Alice's side window came a demand from the partiers. "Hey Jeff," Spinga's voice rings out through the group at the open window, "The party has started, get over here."

Jeff cringed at the intrusion and his inability to drown it out. "Okay, Spinga, I'll be over in a minute." He looked over at Marilyn's chair, 'It wasn't going to come anyway, Marilyn, you know as well as I that I've written myself into a box and I can't get out.' Without the slightest desire to party, Jeff pushed his chair forward to the desk, said goodbye to Marilyn and headed to the party.

His first thought upon entering was to get a drink so he could handle the noise. Within just a few steps Karen Sawyer stopped him, "I hear that you and Alice's friend, Joan, went on a picnic together… I would like to go on a picnic with you."

"It was a business picnic, Karen. I really need a drink to relax. Maybe we can talk more about this later." Jeff smiled and moved another few steps, and was stopped again. This time by Sara Labelle, a librarian, who works for the city of Tomington. She gave him a giant hug. "I haven't seen you for a while Jeffrey, maybe we could go see a movie."

Hi Sara, "I'm in the middle of this book, and I'd like to finish it before I do anything else."

"Oh, it doesn't have to be this week, but I would really like to go with you, maybe, next week?" Jeff fakes a smile and continues to the bar. Joan, observed the two neighbors swooning over Jeff, as he made his way to the bar. "Spinga, could you make me a mild high ball?"

"You're not ordering scotch?" Joan asks with a grin. Jeff turned around hesitantly.

"No, I'm going to keep it light tonight."

"That's good… I want to apologize for cutting you off so abruptly at our picnic. I just got so frustrated with myself for not helping you get on track with the book." Spinga listened to every word hoping to join in the conversation, but other drinkers were impatient for refills, so he reluctantly turned away and helped them. Mark Mitchell, a late arrival, along with the girls across the street, Jamie and Carly were the last to show.

The girls quickly came up to Jeff, and said their hello. "I thought maybe you girls were avoiding me."

"Hardly," responded Carly. In fact, we took our car out of the garage already so we could take you to the festival." Jamie, acting a little quiet, agreed with Carly. "Thanks for the invitation, but I may want to come home early, so I better take mine."

Carly insisted, "If you want to come home early, it'll be fine. Either way."

"Okay, but I'm not much into the festive mood this year." Alice was serving finger food around to the guests, when she nudged Jeff from the back, "You going to save me a dance tonight?"

"You know I can't dance to Jazz." She gave a dejected look, and Jeff quickly changed his tune. "Alice for you I will make an exception." The girls were reaching for Alice's finger food when Jamie whispered to Alice, "Could we talk a little business before we leave?"

"Tonight?"

"It's very important, Alice," responded Carly.

"Everyone is beginning to leave. Why don't we go into the dining room?" The girls never acted this way before and it gave Alice an eerie feeling. The three sat at the dining table and Carly began to explain, "We understand that your house guest is looking for a home. Would she be interested in buying ours?"

"I don't know for sure, but she thought you two had the style home she wanted. In fact, when she told me that last night, I began searching the computer, for that style."

"We want you to handle the selling of our home. Everything stays."

"Even all your antiques?"

"Everything." Jamie responded nervously.

"I hate to do this sale for you girls because I don't want you to leave."

"If you don't, we'll get someone else, and we don't want to do that," threatened Jamie.

Alice was surprised and somewhat nonplused that the girls were not explaining why such a drastic change in their life style was about to happen, but she respected their wishes and didn't ask any more questions.

In a few minutes everyone was clamoring out the door and Alice locked it behind her. Alice shouted, "Now who is going with who, or whom is going with whom?" With a beautiful night and a sixty-degree forecast until mid-night, Spinga lowered the top on his 88 Oldsmobile and looked around for women. "Hey Karen and Sara, how about coming with Mark and me? It'll be like a double date. Mark, you can pick up your car later."

Karen gave a look of shear torture then accepted. Sara, not wanting to be left alone for the night, also accepted. Mark held the seat forward so Karen could get in, then quickly stepped in front of Sara and sat in the back seat. Sara gave Mark a look of contempt, then sat in the front passenger seat. Spinga tapped the seat next to him, "These are bench seats, you can snuggle next to me." Sara glanced over at Jeff and the girls and thought, 'I'm with this guy and you guys have space in your car?' Spinga quickly accelerated, fearing they might change their minds.

"Jeff, do you want to go with Joan and me?" asks Alice.

"I'm going with the girls. I already warned them that I may be poor company and want to go home early." The girls assured Alice that they were not looking forward to a long night, so Alice and Joan made their way around the house to the garage and followed the others to Goshen County Fairgrounds.

When the group arrived and heard the blaring music coming from the hall, it was like their adrenalin drove them to drink. In short order the party goers seemed to be downing drinks at a clip that would make for some bad hangovers tomorrow. By eleven p.m. Spinga had only been slapped twice for inappropriate behavior by Sara.

Mark was so enthralled by Karen's beauty that he was more like her puppy dog than her match. Alice was having an unusually good time talking with business acquaintances. Jeff sat quietly with the girls making small talk. Joan, sat across the table, totally bored and ready to go home. Carly raised her hand for another round of drinks. Jeff pulled her hand down. "I'm done after this one… If you want more, go ahead. I'll find somebody else to take me home."

Jamie leaned near to Jeff's ear so he could hear clearly over the music, "You haven't danced with Alice yet."

"She's preoccupied. I don't think she has given it another thought." Jamie squirmed showing disgust. "What's the big deal Jamie?" Carly smiled at Joan, then asked, "Why don't you and Jeff dance."

Joan stood up quickly gestured to Jeff, "I thought you would never ask." The two went out on the dance floor. Alice, still interested in her company of friends, watched the two dance together. One of Alice's friends remarked, "They dance well together."

When the dance ended, Jamie handed Jeff his old drink. He pushed it aside. "I'm done." Carly pushed it back to him to finish. He downed it remarking that he was ready to leave.

When Joan asked if she could have a ride back to Alice's, the girls looked as though they were deer in the headlights. Jamie jumped up and said, "Okay, but let's go right now." They all stood up. Jeff was going to say goodbye to Alice when Carly grabbed his arm and yelled across the floor to Alice, "We're leaving." Alice headed over to say goodbye, when she saw them hastily filing out the door.

Arriving at Alice's door, they let Joan out. Jeff started to get up but sat back down out of dizziness. Surprised, Joan reached for Jeff's hand to help him out of the car. "We'll take care of him Joan. He must have had one too many. He has done this before.

Joan watched as Carly and Jamie helped Jeff to his front door. Joan shouted to the three, "Good night!"

A second later Carly came out of the house and drove her car to her garage. Then she hurried back to Jeff's house, peaking over at Alice's, fearing that Joan might still be awake, then went on into the house.

Jamie was sitting next to Jeff on the couch and Carly too, hurried to the couch. "So what do we do now?" asks Jamie.

Carly whispers, "Hush, I'm thinking." They're both gaping at Jeff, then Jamie kissed him on the lips. Jeff reached for Jamie for more. They look at each other as to say, it's a go. The two walk Jeff to his bedroom and Carly leaves the two alone. After nearly an hour, Jamie comes out of the bedroom, looking disheveled and exhausted. "So how did it go? He kept saying Marilyn. It's almost haunting. He doesn't stop. He's like a machine."

"Should I go in there and double our chances of success?" Jamie put her head down and didn't answer. Carly, went for it, and headed for the bedroom.

At three a.m. Carly opened the bedroom door and called Jamie to the bedroom. The two covered Jeff's nude body and Jamie checked his pulse. "He's through."

"What do you mean he's through?" Carly began to cry. "No, I mean he's sleeping."

"Jamie, quit using that kind of language!"

Spinga and Mark had just pulled in to pick up Marks car, when they saw Alice coming home. The two sat in Spinga's car discussing what the two did wrong by failing to finish the night with their dates. "Hey, Mark, why don't we try to take Alice out?" The two looked at each other and began to laugh at their chances of every getting a date with her. Suddenly they were spooked at the front door of Jeff's house. They squinted trying to make out who was leaving, then realized it was Carly and Jamie.

The two left Jeff's house not even realizing that Alice had gotten home a few minutes earlier and was coming from her garage to the front door. She saw the girls coming out of Jeff's house, headed for their house, unaware that Alice was standing just yards away. Alice went in the front door to check on Jeff. Nervously she yelled, "Jeff, are you here." No answer. She walked to his bedroom, opened the door, then stepped over to his bed. She stared at him for a minute not knowing what to do, then she touched his jaw. "Jeff, are you okay?" He moaned, then reached for Alice as though he wanted her in bed with him. She pulled away, and whispered roughly, You've had too much to drink. Goodnight." She left still wondering why the girls were with him for three hours after they left the dance.

Mark and Spinga sat quietly, wondering what would happen next. This was exciting and even more fun than taking their so-called dates for nightcaps. "What do you think, Spinga, is Jeff holding out on his extracurricular activities with us?" The two sat with big smiles. Then decided they would play dumb about what they saw. They gave each other a brotherhood handshake. "Let's leave slowly and quietly, declared Spinga. Spinga started his car after Mark left for his own, and began a slow U turn until, fear of getting caught got the better of him, and he gunned it, fish tailing all over the road. Mark panicked at the commotion of the blown plan and gunned his car, creating a double U turn before steering his car straight and heading down the street at full throttle.

Josh arrived promptly at ten the next morning and walked to the back door. He opened the door and called, "Hey, dad, you ready?" He heard Alice's voice coming from the bedroom. When he got to the bedroom door he knocked. "Can I come in?"

"Of course you can come in, what do you think we're doing in here?" Josh turned red faced with his imagination going wild, and found Alice sitting on a chair fully clothed next to the bed.

"What happened to dad?"

"I'm not sure."

"Is he suffering from a hang over?"

"Joan, the one staying at my house, said he only drank a little."

Josh leaned over and shook his dad, then pulled the blankets back like his dad did when he was a child. "Oops", seeing he was naked, he quickly threw the covers back on. Alice turned away, but not fast enough. Jeff moaned, then looked at Alice, "What is going on here?"

"My head is splitting like a jack hammer is trying to break it in two." Alice went to the kitchen and came back with some Tylenol and a glass of water. "What time is it."

"It's ten-thirty, dad."

"I'm so sorry, son, could you tell Charlotte, maybe another time."

"Her name is Cheryl, dad."

"Why don't you examine your dad, and find out what happened last night."

"I'm not an M.D., Alice, I'm studying biological science."

"Just check him, Josh.

He grabbed his dad's wrist for his pulse rate. Waited a minute watching his watch. "Dad, your pulse rate is a hundred and two. He looked into his father's eyes. "My best guess is that you were drugged. Probably, last night." Alice never said a word.

"Son, you better go to Bridgeport without me." Jeff apologized repeatedly, until Josh said "Enough Dad. I forgive you… and the person who wanted to take you home last night." Alice, stared almost glassy-eyed at Josh and Jeff. "Oh Alice, I don't mean you were the woman."

With a labored smile she said, "I didn't think you meant me, at all." Josh got up to leave and couldn't resist, "By the way dad, Alice saw you nude, when I flipped the covers back." Josh walked out of the room trying to whistle and grin at the same time. For the past year, Josh had been trying to plant the seed that his mother had wanted sowed; for those two to end up together.

Jeff looked at Alice, then he lifted the cover slightly and discovered he was nude. Alice left her chair abruptly trekking for the door. "Uhh… what did you think?"

"You were very hard, I mean you were firm, I mean... I don't know what I mean. What can I say, you look very healthy… Ahh gee, I'm going home!"

"You have red flushing forming on your neck, Alice." She rushed through the bedroom door and out the back, taking a deep breath of air, going straight to her patio chair. She sat down with a sigh, then rubbed her red neck. She raised her hand to her forehead to feel her temperature. It felt like she was running a temp. Telling herself over and over to settle down, she finally sat back in the recliner and looked up at the sky. "Please, Marilyn, forgive me. I didn't want to look, but curiosity got the best of me and I couldn't resist. I will never do that again." Breaking into tears, she clutched her hands. "Jeff is yours just like Sam was mine and they are not replaceable."

She left the decking chair to go for a walk and think about all that had happened in the last twenty-four hours. This led her to the girls' house down the street. After thinking about not visiting, she self-consciously went anyway. She rehearsed what she was going to say on her approach to the door. But her rehearsal words were not coming out like her thoughts. This was going to be a futile mistake, but she rang the doorbell, anyway. After a minute of running questions through her brain about what she was going to ask, she realized that the girls were not answering.

She rang again, and again, then stepped away from the door and headed home. She told herself on the way home, It's probably a good thing that they weren't home because she didn't have a clue about what to say of their leaving Jeff's at three in the morning.

When Alice got to the steps of her house, she gave another look back to see if the girl's, maybe woke up, and were wondering who was knocking, but it was still quiet. Taking her five steps up to the porch, she saw a large envelope stuck on the top of her mailbox. It was marked Alice: confidential.

She took, the rather thick envelope, into the house and checked to see where Joan was before opening. Joan was out doing her stretches, but not knowing how long she would work out what with a hangover from last night, she went to the upstairs bathroom.

When Alice went to open the envelope, she saw the girls' names and address sticker, sealing the opening. Dumping everything out on the counter top she looked at each item; garage door opener, three keys, and a box of fish food. Then she unfolded a letter:

> *Dear Alice;*
>
> *You have become our dearest friend in the world. We cherished the times when you and Sam would invite us over along with Marilyn and Jeffrey. We loved the four of you so much that whenever we'd get home, all we'd talk about was how sore we were from laughing.*
>
> *When Sam left this world, we prayed for you every night. When Marilyn went through pain and suffering for a whole year, she was still so gracious. We pray for the four of you every night.*
>
> *We spoke with you about the sale of our house. Whatever we get for it, we know you will do your*

best. If you choose not to deal with us, after reading this letter, we'll understand.

You can contact: J.J. Heil & Associates, in Los Angeles; our address is: Carly & Jamie Willeton, 1369 3rd St., Los Angeles, CA. We hope you will want to communicate with us, even after we tell you what happened, last night.

For the last year we have been trying to adopt a baby, with no luck. When a person becomes desperate, they think of every avenue, and finally we chose the only thing we could do, even though it meant breaking the law... We went to New York a short time ago and made our last ditch effort to adopt. It was all negative.

We met this caseworker at the clinic for adoption. He suggested we start asking any man we saw and offer him money for his semen. That was out of the question. How would we know how healthy this person was or anything else that may haunt us later? The caseworker gave us a name of a guy who had helped others with the same problem. We bought his product and came home. A day later, we went to Jeff and pleaded with him to donate his semen. He, of course, was so understanding about our request, but it was out of the question for him.

Our only hope was the drug that we purchased. We searched the web to find out the side effects and the dangers, of its use. Major hangover was the big side effect. From there, we broke the law and spiked Jeff's drink at the dance, last night.

Alice, we realize that you can turn us in, and we will understand your contempt for us if you never forgive us, but we beg of you to give yourself time to try and understand how desperate we became. Get in touch with us about our home. Pray for us, Alice.

Very truly,
Carly and Jamie

Alice quickly inserted the letter in the envelope, then rushed to her bedroom and deposited it into her safe in the closet. Her mind was telling her to go over to Jeff's house now and make sure he was alright. She ran down the stairs, grabbed the corner banister post, giving her a quick twist toward the back yard.

Joan was startled by the door swinging open so fast, that she stepped back. "What's wrong Alice?" Alice, momentarily was caught off guard, not remembering that she had a house guest. "I was just going over to check on Jeff to see how he was."

"I'll go with you."

"It's really not necessary, Joan, I'm coming right back." Alice continued to Jeff's door without so much as a pause to look back at Joan. She rushed in and called out to Jeff as she approached his bedroom door. "Yes, Alice, I'm in here. What's wrong?"

"Nothing. Are you feeling better?"

"Somewhat, but I would sure like to know what happened to me... Do you have any idea? I had so many dreams about Marilyn, it seemed so real."

"Let's not go into that now." Jeff started to lay back down when Alice stopped him with her arm on his shoulder. "Why don't you take a shower and come over for lunch. Joan would like that. I want to talk to you about something." Alice left the room fast, thinking Jeff might forget he had no clothes on, and jump out of bed.

When Jeff walked in Alice's back door, he saw Joan's luggage near the door. "Hello, I'm here!"

"We're in the kitchen," shouted Alice. When Alice yelled Jeff grasped his head with two hands as though it were going to split. He stepped lightly to the kitchen. Joan pulled the plates from the lower cabinet and looked up at Jeff, "You look like you were hit by a train… Did you have that much to drink?" Alice quickly cut the conversation off and suggested everyone sit and eat. "Jeff, I made your favorite, meat loaf and mashers." Alice placed the meatloaf platter in the center of the table and the three sat down. "I'm not very hungry, Alice."

"You sure didn't look that bad last night, compared to now," remarked Joan. Jeff gave a half grin, then started to eat some mashers. Alice sighed, and cut a few strips of meat loaf for them, then changed the subject. "So, Jeff, are you going to your Literary Awards Banquet in New York next month?" Jeff grunted, "Have you ever known me to go in all these years?"

"No, but maybe you should go. It might help your thought processes get in gear."

"They're giving you an award and you're not going? I wished somebody would honor me for my achievements in my field."

"Tell him Joan. Shouldn't he go? Maybe it would break the rut he's in, and help his writers block?"

"I think Alice is right. As your therapist, I suggest you go and take all of us with you." Jeff sat silent while playing with his food and eating very little. Jeff could not stand the word "Therapist." "Jeff, I was only joking about taking us with you. But, you should seriously think about going. You need a change, and that might trigger something in your head."

Alice got up and started clearing the table. Jeff and Joan began to get up when Alice told both of them to stay seated. "I have something to say to both of you… It'll only take a minute for me to put the dishes in the sink and put the leftovers in the fridge. The two looked at each other rather puzzled.

In a few minutes, Alice sat down and was ready to speak. Joan felt sure she was going to get a lecture about her unprofessional conduct involving Jeff and his problem. Jeff had no clue what Alice was going to say.

Alice hesitated for a minute trying to find the best words to use in describing the last twenty-four hours, without giving up the confidential information from the girls. Jeff could see that this was really troubling Alice, so he decided to start the questioning. "Is it something I said, or was it seeing me nude in bed this morning?" Joan's eyes widened as she began to laugh, "Oh, Alice are you hiding something here?" Alice ignored the remark.

"It's not that. It's much more serious… The girls have moved out of Connecticut."

"You mean the girls are planning on moving?"

"No, they already have."

"That's crazy, Alice. They never said a word about that to me. Where'd they go? Why are they leaving in the first place? They're happy here and I don't understand why they'd up and leave from one day to the next," Jeff exclaimed.

"Well, they have, and now it's up to me to sell their home."

"What's the price they're asking?" inquired Joan.

"It's going to be appraised, including the furnishings. They have a lot of antiques, so the appraisal will take time."

Joan excitedly looked at Alice, "I would love to buy it. Could I call them and make an offer after I look it over?"

Alice quickly responded, "I was given orders to handle the sale for them… I thought you wanted to eventually live near the water at a beach house and not spend too much money on a house in Litchfield?"

Jeff was incredulous, "This is crazy Alice. Something had to have happened to make them literally run away? Now what is it? Did they lose their jobs?" Joan just sat quietly listening to every word. Alice could see that Joan was using her God given instincts and it was time to change the subject again.

"Are you saying that I'll never see them again, but you will be doing business with them?" Jeff asked.

"I'll probably be doing the sale transaction through a San Francisco lawyer," she answered.

"Does that mean they're moving to San Francisco?" Alice thought for a second, "No this law firm handles business transactions all over the country." Jeff got up from the chair, visibly upset, said his good-byes to Joan and Alice, and retired to his study to work on Marilyn's book and forget about his disappointment.

Later that afternoon, Jeff could hear Alice starting her car on the other side of the house and saw her backing it up to the front door. It was visible now and Jeff, from his study, could see Joan put her luggage in the back seat, and she open her door. He lifted the window and Joan turned to wave goodbye. She threw him a kiss. He responded with a subtle wave and smile. She shouted to him, "I hope I'll return as your new neighbor soon." He mumbled to himself, "God help me."

CHAPTER 6

The Awards Banquet

Alice did everything by the book in selling the girls' home. She took three appraisals on the home and property, including three reputable antique dealer appraisals, leaving Joan and the girls very pleased with the final price. Joan had no qualms about the price even though it was hefty, which led Alice to the conclusion that Joan was eager to be near Jeff no matter what. Alice was concerned about Joan being right there on top of her and Jeff on a daily basis. But in the first few weeks, Joan showed her skills as a professional, not to be pushy in analyzing his needs, although her interest in Jeff seemed to be growing. She worked at trying to give him space to solve his writing problems.

With Thanksgiving nearing, and the weather beginning to change to the brrrs of winter, there was less jogging time for the two. When the weather was right, the two took the opportunity to go outside and run. Jeff's morning jogs were seldom alone now, except when Joan was in New York City taping her television shows as a Clinical Psychologist for one week out of each month. The neighbors loved having a television celebrity in neighborhood. Jeff was old news to them and besides all Jeff did was sit at a typewriter and write. She on the other hand, was a glamorous T.V. star so they could actually give their opinions on how she should have responded to the TV guests. Sometimes the first taping would be on the air before she even got home, so they had plenty to talk to her about.

Jeff was prepared to begin his morning jog when he came out the front of his house and did his stretch exercises, looking down the street to see if Joan was coming from her new house... No Joan. Alice had already gone to work, so she couldn't be over there, he thought. He began to jog down the street, but hesitated, turned around and headed to Joan's house.

He stood knocking at her door waiting for her to answer, paused, finally, after his second knock, she came to the door. "Yes, who's there?"

"It's me, Jeff. You going to go jogging today?"

"No, Jeff, I don't feel well."

"Could you open the door, maybe I can help you?"

"No Jeff, I don't want you to get my flu bug."

"Don't worry about me, I'm much tougher than that."

She opened the door. She never wanted Jeff to see her without makeup and being sick, to boot. He smiled, "You look a mess."

"Thanks, Jeff, I really needed a second opinion."

"How'd you catch this terrible cold?"

"Probably from jogging with you yesterday."

"If I'm the cause of your misery, then it's only right that I bring you back to health."

"I was just kidding with you. Go do your morning workout." Jeff ignored her suggestion and guided her to her couch. Then he went to the kitchen, found a can of chicken soup, microwaved it, then served it to her on a TV tray. She picked up the spoon, then hesitated.

"What's wrong?"

"Nothing."

"Is it crackers you want?"

"Yes, but don't bother." He was up and back before she finished her sentence.

He went back to the kitchen and fixed a soup bowl for himself. Returning, he sat next to her. "I don't want you to eat alone." She gave him a nudge with her elbow, "You're just too sweet."

When they finished the soup, Jeff took away the bowls, washed them and the other dishes in the sink, then put them away. She smiled at him, when he returned. He sat next to her, waiting for her every need. "I don't want to keep you from your morning Jog."

"I'm staying," He said sternly. She began stretching her body out on the couch when Jeff moved to give her more room. She stopped him. "May I lay my head on your lap?"

Jeff hesitated slightly, "Oh...of course you may." He saw a folded blanket on the high back chair across the room and gently raised her head so he could stand and get it. He unfolded it, draped it over her robe and tucked it around her back, legs and feet. She moaned with thanks. He raised her head and sat back down, placing her head back on his lap. "That's the softest blanket I've ever touched." She closed her eyes with a smile, "It's fleece." Joan drifted in and out of sleep. He felt her forehead; it was very warm. He got up and put a pillow cushion under her head and went to the kitchen to search for a wash rag. Finding one in a drawer next to the forks and knives, he soaked it with cold water, then applied it to Joan's forehead. "Ohhh... that feels like heaven."

"Do you need anything, else?" Joan thought for a second. "Would you hold my hand and tell me what you feel."

"So you want me to do my 'Impulse reactor?'"

"Yes." Jeff was sitting on the edge of the coffee table when he reached for her outstretched hand. He held her hand for a minute.

"What do you feel, Jeff?" "About a hundred thousand flu germs coming at me," laughing. "Just kidding," he sighed, and released her hand… "I feel like you should go to sleep and get well, so I don't make any more stupid jokes." He wasn't playing the game well.

"Do you remember me saying several weeks ago that because I was married four times and they were such bad experiences for me that I would never do it again? Well I…" Jeff cut her off. "I respect your decision and I certainly wouldn't want to change your heart." She wanted to tell him how she was feeling about him, but her psychology experience was telling her to leave it alone. He was not ready.

Jeff held the wash rag to her forehead, then He saw her eyes staring at him, "I have just come to realize, that without makeup, you are a twin to Anna Magnani."

"I don't think I know who that is."

"It's not who she is, but who she was." Jeff never told anybody, but it made sense to tell Joan, for her research…. "My first two books sold very well. I had an agent with connections in Hollywood. He called me and asked if I could write a screenplay of my second book. I of course said sure, even though I had no idea how to write one. Marilyn and I were married for just two months and were never apart for more than an hour at a time, but she said I had to go. So I flew in an airplane, four engine prop job, for the first time, to the West Coast." Joan was not in the mood to hear a story from the past, at this moment, but gave a forced smile for him to continue.

"I met my agent at the Burbank airport, and he drove me to the Brown Derby Restaurant in Hollywood. We were a little late for the meeting, so He made an excuse that the traffic was bad. There were no handshakes when we got to a large booth at the back of the restaurant. The two producers pointed for me to sit across from them, next to an older woman. Two other writers sat at the back of the booth next to her. We were at a ninety-degree angle, so when we turned to each other it was full frontal. For some reason my eyes moved from her face to a picture above her head. It was her picture signed Anna Magnani."

She touched my arm and remarked, "how old are you kid?" 'Not very?' That was such a stupid answer. I left for home never to see her again.

Joan sat up then stood. Jeff quickly stood. "I'm doing much better now, Jeff."

"You want me to go?"

"Yes. Go for your run and don't worry about me."

"I can bring you lunch. I can't bring you dinner tonight because I have to go to Hartford this afternoon, to see my editor. I have to explain why I haven't finished my book. Maybe he has some ideas."

"I'm fine. I just need some time to clear my head cold, so don't bring me lunch. I'm going to sleep the rest of the day." She walked him to the door, said goodbye, then closed the door. She gasped at herself in the round mirror and yelled, "My God, a man saw me this way!" She calmed down in a few seconds, then looked in the mirror again. "I look like a movie star?" She could not understand why she was letting her guard down and falling for this man that she hardly knew. Her heart was pounding, and it wasn't from her cold. She went to her computer to find this actress, Anna Magnani. Eventually realizing what a great actress this Anna was.

Later Jeff called Alice at work and explained Joan's condition. Alice listened as Jeff told her about leaving for Hartford and maybe staying one or two nights. She assured him that she'd check on Joan. Alice had a strange feeling that Jeff was acting like he did when Marilyn got sick. Then she thought about how he was with her, when she became ill. It just may be his nature to care about others, not necessarily that He was falling for Joan.

Jeff was reluctant to meet with Jeremy Sutton, his editor, knowing full well that Jeremy had reserved his time often over the course of two years, to begin the editing process for Jeff's new book. Jeremy didn't show impatience, when the two met. He knew this was Jeff's biggest challenge to date. Jeremy had done the previous ten books for Jeff and they had developed a great respect for each other, over the years.

They met at the Howard Johnson Inn, welcoming each other with a handshake. Sitting down in a quiet spot in the lobby, Jeff began explaining his quagmire. Then handed Jeremy the half-done manuscript. Jeff stared at him as he started thumbing through page after page. Then Jeremy made a suggestion. "Jeff, why don't you go in to the restaurant and have something to eat? You make me nervous watching me."

Jeff grunted a bit, then left, to allow Jeremy to discover what Jeff's problem was in completing this book. In less than ten minutes, Jeremy sat down next to Jeff, placed the manuscript down on the counter without saying a word. Finally, Jeff asked, "So what do you think?"

"After all the enjoyable editing I've done for you, I have never seen you write yourself into a box. This book, is the exception. For the last fifteen years, I have read every chapter, every sentence, and you have never done this before. In your last chapter, you have made it final. Your book is done, it's as far as you can go. It's the end. I read just a few words at the beginning of each chapter and the way you started and ended each chapter gave me the feeling that the last chapter ended your story."

"It's not complete, though."

"Your absolutely right, Jeff, but if I know why its incomplete I would be a writer instead of an editor." Jeff stopped eating his roast beef and put his fork down. "I take it you are not going to solve my problem?"

"I don't know how."

"Should I throw it away?"

"You cannot throw this away. You know it and I know it... I am going to give you my honest opinion: I think you have written a goodbye to Marilyn, and a goodbye to writing for yourself." Jeff looked away, then turned back to Jeremy. "You're telling me, I'm done as a writer, but then you tell me I have to complete this. You're not making any sense." Jeff called the waitress over, "Ma'am, could I have a glass of water? I'm dying of thirst." She brought him his water and he quickly downed the full glass. She put the bill down on the counter and Jeff put a twenty-dollar bill on it. "Keep the change. You're a very fine person, unlike my editor here."

"Thank you very much Mr. Williams... May I ask you for a favor?" Jeff smiled realizing she knew his name and that usually meant they want something for nothing. "Would you sign my book... or, rather your book, "Connecticut Cove"?" Jeff signed it, then handed it back to her almost ready to apologize for thinking she wanted something for nothing. "What's the title of your next book?"

"Forever Yours, Marilyn" or something like that.

"Who's the lucky woman?"

"My wife." Jeremy broke into the conversation and she walked away clutching the book to her chest. "I'm trying to be honest with you, Jeff. You may not be done as a writer, but something in you has to change. I could be wrong and I hope I am, but whichever way it works out and you finish it, I would be honored to edit this book at no charge."

"Thanks Jeremy. I'm going to make some changes in what I'm doing, I'm just not sure what they are. I have a neighbor friend who is a psychologist, and she talked to me about my problems. I wrote down a lot of notes after we spoke. You know me about taking notes and studying them later."

"Hopefully, she can help you. For all the books you've written you probably should have a shrink nearby." Jeff looked at his watch, totally ignoring Jeremy. "I don't think I'm staying here tonight; I'm going to go see Josh at his college. He's always saying I never visit him up there."

"That's good. Change your routine." The two said their good-byes and Jeff headed up highway 44 to Storrs. Jeff grabbed his cell phone to call Josh, but realized he had forgotten to charge it. Marilyn was always having to remind him of little things that he neglected to do.

It was nearly nine p.m. when Jeff got to Josh's driveway. He pulled up alongside a blue Camaro and parked. He grabbed his overnight bag and went to the door. His knock on the door brought a quick yell, "Who is it?" It was a female voice. Jeff thought for a second, wishing he had not come, or at least had a charged phone, so he could have called. "I'm Jeff, Josh's father."

Josh shouted, "I'll be right there Dad." He could hear whispers and a lot of pattering of feet. When Josh finally opened the door, Jeff responded, "Did I catch you at a bad time, son?"

"No, dad. We had to clean the place a little before we let you in."

"So, where's the girl?"

"What girl?"

"The one who answered my knock. The one you said 'we' had to clean the room before answering. Was that Charlotte?"

"Dad, I don't know a Charlotte, it was Cheryl."

"So where is she?"

"Cheryl, could you come out here?" Cheryl came from the bedroom still touching up her hair. Josh's cheeks were solid red. Jeff knew that Josh was caught in a compromising position, much like when his mother was guilty of something, no matter how trivial it was, her cheeks would go blush. "Dad, this is Cheryl. Cheryl, this is my dad who should have called before dropping in."

"My phone went dead."

"It wouldn't have, if you had remembered to charge it. I don't know how many times mom warned you about charging that stupid thing."

"I'd better go. I'll find a motel, then head home tomorrow."

"Cheryl and I were getting ready to go out for pizza. How would you like to join us?"

"Well, I am starving, I haven't eaten for a long stretch." Jeff sighed slightly, wondering where he would fit pizza in his stomach after eating a hot roast beef sandwich just one hour ago. But he really wanted to get to know Josh's girlfriend better. After all, he thought, Josh is getting to that age where this might be the one he would marry, so it's important for a dad to give his non-biased, life experiences, for his son's wellbeing.

The three hopped into Jeff's Jag, then Josh gave his dad driving instructions to Storrs Champion Pizza. A typical college hangout with banners draped all over the walls commemorating the championship teams that the University of Connecticut had won. It was a little noisy for Jeff, but he smiled and endured. They ordered a combo pepperoni. Cheryl excused herself and went to the lady's bathroom.

"She doesn't say much, does she, son?"

"Are you judging her already, dad?"

"No, but you remember how you always said your type of girl was somebody outdoorsy and who liked animals."

"So how do you know she doesn't like horses, cows, dogs, cats, and anything else from the animal kingdom, you just met her?" Jeff hesitated for a minute not wanting to get Josh upset and yet wanting to prove his point. "She has long nails. They're painted a terrible looking blue, and she doesn't talk very much. In fact, she has not uttered a word since you introduced her to me."

"Have you thought maybe she's quiet because she doesn't know you?"

"No." Cheryl came out of the restroom and stopped to talk to some guy friends, standing near the bar. Then headed for her table.

"Okay dad, she's coming now be nice." They both stood slightly as she sat down. "So, did the two of you talk about me while I was gone?" The two looked at each other and shook their heads no, as if incredulous to the question.

When the waiter brought the pizza, the father and son waited for Cheryl to pull her piece from the tray. Jeff watched as she carefully maneuvered her hand, trying not to crack a nail and slowly placed it on her plate. Jeff smiled, "Those are sure long fingernails, you have there."

"Yes they are, Mr. Williams, and I plan on keeping them that way."

"How do you pick up a cat or pet dog?" Josh was beginning to show his disgust when Cheryl answered, "I don't have a dog or a cat, and I don't plan on having any." Josh was surprised at her response and asked, "You don't like animals?"

"Animals are fine, but not for me."

"Well, I'm sure we can work around that, eventually."

"No, it's not now and it's not later. In fact, Josh, you can entertain your dad alone because my friends over at the bar are going home to Bridgeport tonight and I'm going home with them." She stands from her chair. "Goodbye." Abruptly, she threw her overcoat on and she and her guy friends were out the door.

"How do you do it, dad?"

"Well, son, it's like writing. You have to figure all the scenarios that could or should happen in a story and pick the best direction. It's similar to a chess game."

"No, no, dad. I don't mean it in a good way. I've been going with Cheryl for several months. We have been getting along just fine, no arguments, or disagreements, then in one hour she meets you and she's gone from me.

"I'm sorry son. I didn't mean to intrude in your life. I'm just trying to separate the wheat from the chaff for you."

"Don't go biblical on me, dad." The two got up from the table, Josh waved to the waiter for a box to take the remainder of the pizza home. Jeff drank a full glass of water and complained that the pizza must have been spicy so they could sell more beer, then headed for Josh's apartment.

Josh convinced his dad to stay one more night so he could read his dad's unfinished novel. The two enjoyed a couple rounds of golf the next morning and enjoyed each other's company. When Josh finished the novel on Friday evening, he placed the novel on his dad's suitcase. "So what did you think of it?"

Josh smiled with tears in his eyes, "Mom was such a great person. I miss her so much." Jeff could see the emotions that were taunting Josh's memory and his dad's written words. "You may be right about Cheryl, but I have to figure these things for myself, although I do want your kind of marriage."

"Be patient, son. I'll find somebody for you." Jeff went to the fridge for a bottled water.

"Thanks, dad, but I can find someone myself, and what's the deal with all the water you're drinking?"

Saturday morning, Jeff woke up to a bad headache and an aching body. He ditched his plan to go jogging and instead packed his things and was ready to leave the minute Josh woke up. He sat at the kitchen table drinking a fresh cup of coffee that made him feel even worse. "Hey Josh! I'm going home son." Josh quickly jumped out of bed and put a pair of pants on and made his way into the kitchen. "Wow, dad, you don't look very good. You look almost like when you were drugged at the Jazz Festival."

"I don't know if I was actually drugged or what!"

"Trust me dad you were drugged... maybe you shouldn't travel in this condition." With a wry smile, Jeff turned to his son, "Son, if I am to die this day, it will be in my own house."

"Who said that, a founding father?" Josh carried his dad's overnight bag to the car and the two, said goodbye.

Jeff began his hour drive home wishing he was already home in bed. It took longer than an hour because of frequent stops to close his eyes and rest. When he pulled into the driveway, he could not believe he was actually home. Without even taking his luggage out, he headed for bed.

He had begun stripping off his clothes, when the phone rang. He looked at it, like it was a noise monster. His intention was to let it ring and just climb into bed. But the persistence finally got the better of him and he answered it. "Hello." A voice at the other end spoke. "Hello Jeff, this is Joan. Your son called Alice and told her you weren't feeling well and she called me from work to tell me to check on you.

"Thank you Joan for checking on me, now goodbye." He dropped the phone on the floor and crawled into bed. He couldn't believe he was home and in his own bed. It only took a moment when he realized the phone was humming a busy tone. "My God, would somebody hang that stupid phone up?"

It was still sounding a busy tone when Joan entered the back door. She yelled for Jeff, but no response. She went into his bedroom and found the phone and placed it on the holder stopping that awful deafening sound. Jeff moaned, "Thank you." She sat on the edge of his bed, staring at him. "So how bad do you feel?"

"You know how you felt the other day? Well I'm ten times worse." Joan couldn't hold back her smile. "What are you smiling about, I'm dying here and you think it's funny?"

"I thought you were this tough guy who never gets sick."

"Please Joan, let a man die in peace."

"I would not think of letting you die alone. I'll remain here until your death." In short order Jeff was fast asleep, but Joan remained with him for the next three hours. When she got up to leave, Jeff raised his head. "Thanks Joan for caring about me... On second thought, you were the one that gave me this near death sentence, so you owe me. Joan leaned over and gave him a kiss on his forehead. "What was that for?" She gave him a pinch on his cheek. "I was just checking to see if you had a temp. I think you'll live."

"Joan? I would like to invite you to go to New York along with Alice and my other friends to my award banquet, if you'd like to come?"

"I thought you didn't like awards?"

"My editor, along with my shrink, thinks I need to change my life, by getting out and doing things."

"I would be honored to go as your friend." She kissed him on his forehead again.

"Now what was that for?"

"I was just checking to see if your fever was influencing your brain... and thanks for inviting me. I would love to go."

CHAPTER 7

Thanksgiving, was just days away. With morning hard freezes and the day high's in the low forties, morning jogs were out for Jeff or for Joan when she was home. Jeff found himself trapped in his house more now, and was looking for ways to fight the boredom. His biggest enjoyment was taking one of Marilyn's books from the shelf, sitting in her chair, and reading it from cover to cover.

Her words resonated in his mind as though she were sitting in the room with him. He would smile when he got to an especially clever set of words that she worked hard to generate. She would not except a lessor meaning of words to convey a sentence, unlike the way he wrote. His approach was that his first thoughts were the best, and it was unnecessary to rack his brain for other descriptive words when what he wrote would suffice. That's what was so special about her, he thought… a need for perfection.

When he finished her book, he closed it, slowly, fighting tears. "I love you Marilyn." He looked around the room observing all the added pictures on the walls, then leaned back in his chair wondering what he could read next. His eyes fixed on the legal pad that sat alone on the book cabinet near the doorway. He stared at it for a second, then got up and brought it back to his chair to read.

He labeled the notes: Joan's Evaluation of Me. The first page didn't make a lot of sense, but when he got to the second, it made him think. Her questions seemed to have more of an impact now that he was reading from his notes. The more he reread, the more he could see a pattern in her questions. She was telling him to let go. Let Marilyn go.

He didn't want to, but it was becoming more apparent, that he must. His life was being ravaged by memories. The question was how would he accomplish this. Is it time, he asked himself? Was it leaving Connecticut, for another place to live? Or, maybe finding another person to share his life with? He couldn't make this decision without visiting Marilyn's and Jodie's home for good, and feel the Montana sky come into his heart and soul.

The clock rang at five a.m. Jeff jumped out of bed and headed for the shower. He had packed his bag the night before for the trip to New York to receive his literary award. At seven a.m. the phone rang. Jeff quickly answered it to stop the nuisance ring. The sound of a ringing phone brought instant fear that the message he would hear was tragic news of death of someone he knew. "Hello."

"Hi Jeff, this is Alice, we're ready to go. Everyone is here."

"I've been thinking, Alice, I'm not too sold on attending."

"Hold on, Jeff, I'm sending Joan over to speak with you."

"No. You don't have to send her over."

"Too late Jeff, she's on her way." Alice put the phone down and the rest of the party sat waiting for Joan to do her magic work. On her little trek over to Jeff's, she worked on a plan of attack. Without knocking, she entered and went straight up to Jeff. "Are you going to let down all those people at Alice's house? They have been planning this trip for weeks."

"What, is this some kind of guilt trip on me? I'm not saying the trip would be off for you guys. I'll still pay for everything and you guys can go without me.

"It's not only you that is affected by your decision, they've changed their schedules so they could be with you and celebrate your award. The trip is meaningless without you." Jeff reached for his legal pad.

"I have looked over my notes, that I wrote down from your shrink sessions with me. I'm thinking about a trip to visit Marilyn in Missoula." He waited for a response from Joan. It was slow in coming, then she remarked, "I think that is a good idea. It also doesn't mean you can't do both, your trip to New York and Missoula."

"Okay, you're right of course, I should be going and enjoying myself with my friends. "The limo driver called at six-thirty to say he'd be here at seven." Joan looked at her watch, then glanced out the side window hearing a car. He has just arrived. So let's go before you have another mood swing." Joan grabbed his two suits that were on hangers and Jeff picked up his bag, then the two left out the back door with Joan nudging him to keep moving. "I can carry my own suits… I hope everybody followed my one bag rule, otherwise we may be stacking bags on the roof of the car."

"Yes… and another thing, do you have to wear a suit now? Wouldn't you be more comfortable with jeans?"

"It never occurred to me." She just shook her head. Joan yelled to Alice that the limo was there. They all came out, each carrying one bag. The limo driver smiled and asked, "Who enforced the one bag rule on all you guys?"

"The guy in the suit, muttered Karen Sawyer."

"I didn't think you guys would follow my suggestion. I'm bringing extra suits on hangers."

Karen sighed, realizing they were all were careful not to upset Jeff. The driver stuck two smaller bags on the front seat, then the rest went into the trunk. "Okay, ladies and gentlemen, my name is Francisco, giving a wink to Spinga. Mark nudged Spinga, "He likes you." I will be driving you to the Roosevelt Hotel in New York City. He handed business cards to Jeff, Alice and Karen. "If you want me to drive you guys around town after you settle into your rooms, you call me on my cell. Now, does anybody have to go to the restroom before we leave?" Alice quickly excused herself and went back in her house. "It works every time I ask," declared Francisco. He opened the side door and Karen, wanting to get out of the cold, began to enter. "And your name is?" "Karen Sawyer." He wrote her name on a tablet. "You sure are tall." "I would estimate that I'm a foot taller than you, so watch your approach, fella." "Well, you're a beautiful woman, but sometimes height isn't everything. Next." "My name is Sara Labelle." He jots her name down on the tablet. Alice rushes from the house. Francisco stops her from entering the car. "So what is your name?" "I'm Alice Bates." Again he writes the name. "My name is Mark Mitchell, the grandson of Billy Mitchell, the World War I pilot. Do you know who that is?" "Don't think so. Next." "I'm Spinga Cuoto. I don't have any pilots in my family." "Spinga? That means boney in my home language. My cousin has the same name." Spinga gets in. "My name is Jeff Williams." "Oh, you're da'man. My boss said to be very nice to you. Do you know Benjamin Ford?" "Yes, of course, he's my publisher."

"Huh, I better explain why I take names, so you don't report me for keeping you people out in the cold: Once I had twelve people in the car and I stopped for a restroom break just before the Jersey turnpike. A man and a woman went into a brushy area and did what horny people do. I drove out without them. Fifty miles down the road the group was laughing about the two getting left behind. I had to go back and get them after dumping off the other ten loose screws. Never again."

Sara yelled from inside the car, "You made us wait out in the cold, when we could have been in the warm car and answer the same questions?"

"You should have said something." Everyone looked at each other smiling, accepting the dumbness of not entering when the door was wide open. They sat comfortably, with Alice near the window and Jeff at the other window, with Joan in the middle. Mark and Spinga knew that being strategically located in the limo meant either a great trip or just satisfactory, so they stayed a short arm's length from Sara and Karen.

It wasn't long into the trip, that Jeff became very quiet. He gazed out the window watching the blurring fence posts and the sheep and cattle scratching away the snow so they could forage for grass. Jeff had taken this trip a bunch of times with Marilyn until the two grew tired of the nonsense of awards. The last trip they took to New York was nearing fifteen years before, Marilyn on returning home, sat in her chair in the study and remarked, "Why do we have to receive an award for something we love to do? If our words are good, the reward will be someone taking pleasure in what we wrote. That's my reward." They never went to another award after that.

Alice knew some of what was going through Jeff's mind. She and Sam had made this same trip with them a few times for this same reason. Alice mimed with her fingers, gesturing to Spinga to say something, hoping to break Jeff's silence. Spinga looked around desperately trying to come up with something to remind him of a joke.

Francisco, the driver, dropped his glass window and announced in his feminineness voice, "Mr. Benjamin said you can have any drinks in the ice cabinet you want, and also in the other compartment is a continental breakfast. So help yourselves." That is exactly the thing that may get this weekend rolling, thought Alice. Spinga pulled out a bottle of champagne, held it up, and cheered, "Let the weekend begin."

Seemingly, in minutes, Francisco, with a cheer declared, "We're here." He quickly got out and hustled around the limo to open the door, then pulled the luggage from the trunk. Everyone had exited the car except Spinga and Karen. With the heavily shaded windows Francisco came around to the door to see what the holdup was with the two. They were in a tight clinched position. Francisco turned around with a smile, to address the others. "Let me show you my sticker on the back bumper," telling the group.

They all walked to the back of the limo, not knowing where he was going with this. Then he pointed to the bumper. It read: *I give single people a ride...They go home as a couple.* This happens in my limo all the time. The four still didn't understand the meaning until they walked to the side door and saw Spinga and Karen totally wrapped up in each other.

Alice looked down at the three champagne bottles lying on the floor. "Are you two coming or are you going to the parking garage?" The two looked at her then at each other as if to ponder the options given. Alice yelled, "For heaven's sake, get out of there." It is obvious that you two had too much champagne.

Entering the lobby, the five stopped just past the door. Jeff turned to see what happened to the five. They were staring at the giant banner draped across the wall to the conference hall near the elevator lobby. Mark read it aloud, "Jeffrey Williams Awards Night."

"It doesn't seem like the same Jeff I know from Litchfield," remarked Sara.

"It's the same one", assured Jeff. "Let's check in." Joan walked with him, giving him a look.

"What's the look for, Joan?"

"You are so incredibly modest. Marilyn was such a lucky woman."

"No, Joan, you have that backwards." Jeff was serious, as the group got to the front desk. But when he saw his old friend, Daniel, a smile came to his face. Daniel said, "Hello, Mr. Williams."

"Oh stop being so formal, Danny. Are you the main man around here now?"

"Yes, Jeffrey, I'm the boss. At least that's what the owners say. Sometimes the help doesn't think so because some of them started working here before I did."

Jeff turned to Alice, "Do you remember Danny?"

"Is this the Danny that was a bell hop for us twenty years ago?" Danny smiled, "Yep I'm the same one."

"My husband always said you were the best bell hop he had ever seen." Daniel thought for a second, then decided not to ask where her husband was. "Your publisher, Benjamin Ford pre-booked four rooms for your group. He said they had to be together and that anything your guests want; I am to give it to you." Jeff got the four lock-cards from Danny and handed them out. First card, room 604, he gave to Joan and Alice, the second, room 605 went to Mark and Spinga and the third, room 606 went to Sara and Karen. "I'll be in room 607, by myself, he declared. I never know when my mind might start writing and I may need to be alone."

Joan frowned, "Does that mean if you begin to write just before this awards thing, you'll not show up?"

"If I do that, my publisher will kill me."

They all rode the elevator together, up to the six floor. Everyone was wondering, without a word, just how long it would be before Karen and Spinga would find a way to share a room together. When the elevator stopped, the group hurriedly went to their rooms to freshen up and head out for a crazy Friday afternoon.

When Alice was ready she called Jeff on the hotel phone to invite him for an afternoon of sightseeing. He declined. Alice reverted to her most convincing counterpart, Joan. In two minutes Joan knocked on Jeff's door. Jeff yelled from his desk near the window, "Yes, Joan."

She yelled back, "How'd you know it was me?" Jeff came to the door and opened it.

"Because I know Alice. She'll use every method possible to convince me to relax and have fun, and you seem to be the one that can get to me. Is that a fair assumption?"

"Is that so terrible?"

"No. It's just one of many, of her great attributes. I love Alice as a dear, dear friend." Jeff hesitated for a second… "Do you have a minute to talk?"

"Yes, but Alice called and told Francisco that we'd be ready to go sightseeing in five minutes."

Jeff pulled a chair out from the desk for her, then he sat. She saw at least ten new legal pads on the desk, ready for any words that may come into his head.

"How realistic, in your opinion, is it for me to complete this novel?"

"You can answer that better than me. I think staying in your room like this, and hoping that something comes to you, is a mistake. I'm sorry, but that's what I believe."

"You really mean that, don't you?"

"Put this trip and the trip to Missoula to good use and break this log jam. It may take a week, a month, or even six months. Hopefully not longer, because I would miss you terribly." Jeff got up and walked Joan to the door. Joan said, "Alice said if you didn't go out on the town now, at least make dinner at six, down at the hotel restaurant… and that you better make it. Apparently, she knew you wouldn't change your mind for this afternoon. She knows you like you know her… Jeff, from now on, I cannot give you anymore advice as a professional. I have far too many conflicts of interest to contend with… I don't think it is wise." She opened the door and left, hurriedly hoping she hadn't delayed the others. Jeff stood at the door, momentarily digesting her words. Then he walked to the window to wait for his friends to exit the building.

Francisco pulled up to the curb and barely had time to run and open the door before the group's laughter and chatter could be heard racing to the car. Jeff smiled at his excited friends as they entered the car. Alice started to follow Sara when Joan pulled her arm, "I told Jeff that I couldn't be objective in his problems. I'm looking at him differently."

"He's not ready, Joan. If you really are falling for him, maybe you should let him lead." Alice looked up to the sixth floor then entered the limo. She couldn't see Jeff in the shadows. Jeff knew that Joan said something to her about him. The Limo headed out 45th street amidst all the other limos, taxi's and cars.

Jeff sat down to write his speech for the following night. He sat for nearly an hour waiting for just the right words to put in his notes. The words had to be thought out carefully and carry great wisdom. They had to be words that Marilyn would use. Jeff sat waiting for the crafted words to suddenly gel in his mind and muster the words that great writers would use.

He began to laugh and laugh because nothing was coming from his somewhat vacant brain. "What is it? Have I got Alzheimer's? Could it be my brain is failing to function from over use? Or maybe from underuse?" He stared at his large hotel room and remarked to himself, "What in the world am I even doing here? This is crazy, I don't want to be here, nor do I want this stupid award." Tears started to well up in his eyes from disgust. "I gotta be losing my mind." He pulled the bed spread back and flopped to the pillow. He looked at his wristwatch. "It's only two o'clock," he said to himself, deciding to relax for a couple hours before going to dinner in the hotel restaurant at 6 p.m. He lay on his back feeling the comfort the bed afforded him, and the memories from the past... The smells of the room, the same floor that he and Marilyn always stayed in, and the cars down on the street blasting their horns, were just different cars, but the same type of drivers. The difference; Marilyn was not here.

A light knock on the door, halted a dream of Marilyn, disturbing Jeff and giving polite warning that it was time to stop his writing and come to dinner. When the knock became loader, he awoke. He sat up in bed trying to get his bearings. Then, another knock came with Alice shouting through the door. "Jeff, are you ready for supper?"

Jeff hustled to the door and opened it. "How long have you been sleeping; your eyes are puffy?" Jeff looked at his watch and couldn't believe it was six p.m. already. So much for only wanting to sleep for a couple of minutes, he thought. "I think about four hours. Lately, I seem to fall asleep at the drop of a hat."

"Well you should be well rested. Get dressed and come down to the restaurant… and I don't mean in a suit. If we see you in a suit all the time, you won't look special when it comes time for the awards tomorrow night."

"Alice, I think I'll order room service."

"That's it Jeff. I'm staying here until you take your shower and dress for a sit down dinner."

"You can't stay in my room while I take a shower and dress."

"Don't forget, Jeffrey Williams, I've seen you nude... just take your clothes in the bathroom and get with it." Alice wanted to discuss what Joan said to him before they went sightseeing, but chose not to bring it up. Poor Joan was so embarrassed that she was trying to make excuses for not coming to dinner.

"Is Joan going to dinner?"

"Yes. Why?" Jeff ignored the question and asked his own. "What do you think of Joan?"

"Truthfully, at first I thought she was just a woman who over reacted with men. Her impetuous nature has created some major pitfalls for her. But, seeing her and being around her more this past year, has given me a different perspective on how she thinks. She's a great person who I think would make a great guy, a wonderful wife." He ignored her response.

"Do you remember how the four of us laid claim to who we looked like from Hollywood movies? My question to you is; who does Joan remind you of?"

"I know exactly who she reminds you of, Jeff, it was your favorite, Anna Magnani. Hopefully, you won't be so infatuated that you lose all perspective of the situation."

"Of course not, but think about it; Joan's life is what Anna played in the movies. She was married four times. She lived life to the max. She was her own woman. Magnani's movies 'Wild is the Wind or 'Rose Tattoo' is Joan. Anna died in nineteen seventy-three and she is consanguineous to Joan."

Jeff took his suitcase into the bathroom. Alice walked around his room, checking the time on her watch every few minutes. She checked his window view, then the desk where his note pads lay stacked. One pad sat with a pen near the edge of the table with the title written across the top: *My Acceptance speech.* Alice sat down and wrote: *Maybe you could describe from the beginning, how you got here... without making us cry our hearts out.*

When Jeff came from the bathroom, Alice stood up quickly and moved away from the table.

"Sorry to have taken so long." Alice walked up to him and reached for his throat. "You just had to wear a tie?"

"I'm not wearing a sport suit, okay, just a sweater and tie… in fact it's the same one I wore to the Jazz Festival."

"You need a wife, if for nothing else, to dress you for occasions like these." They both started for the door. "Have we got a story to tell you at dinner." Alice began to laugh at the mere reminiscence of the afternoon.

The two entered the crowded hotel restaurant. Sara stood up and waived to catch Alice and Jeff's attention. When the two got to the table, Sara excitedly asked, "Has Alice told you about our hilarious afternoon?"

"No, not yet." Sara asked, "Who is going to tell Jeff what happened?"

Mark leaned forward in his chair, "Sara, why don't you tell the story about how Karen got this giant lump on her head. So far you've told Francisco, Danny at the front desk, and the cocktail waitress at the bar. It seems to grow crazier every time you tell it."

Sara gave him a squint and then changed it abruptly to a smile, "Okay, I'll tell the story and be totally truthful." The waiter came to the table ready to take their orders just when Sara was about to begin. Jeff looked up to the waiter. "Could you give us a couple more minutes? Sara has a story to tell."

"Sure, just call when you're ready." Sara gestured to Jeff with a thank you smile, for letting her talk without interruptions.

"Okay, Jeff. I'll try to keep this short." Groans came from everyone at the table except Jeff… "We were all in the same department store down the street. It has a lot of nice clothes and we needed a newer wardrobe." Mark and Spinga shifted in their chairs hinting that she was starting to babble. "Karen and

I were shopping on the third floor trying to find better outfits for your awards thing. After putting on a number of outfits, we finally found the ones that seemed the best, but we wanted a second opinion. We headed down the escalator to get Alice and Joan's opinion. When we neared the bottom of the escalator, Karen's dress got stuck in the escalator flipping her on her head, sprawling flat out onto the second floor." Jeff looked to Karen with sympathy.

Spinga interrupted, "I'll take it from here. Mark and I heard the commotion and went to see about all the excitement. Karen was out cold lying on her back with her dress up to her waist." Spinga turned to Karen and remarked, "you do have great looking legs by the way, but that's for a discussion at another time." "Now who's rambling," gestures Sara.

"But here's the funny part," with Spinga struggling to hold his laughter, this large woman who had been trying on bathing suits was in between bathing suits, wearing just a robe. She apparently wanted half-off on the bathing suits because of winter prices. She told everyone to give the poor woman some air straddling Karen's body. "I told the woman that I knew Karen and I wanted to help, but she stretched her arms out gesturing that she was in control. That's when Karen came to and screamed, "I see a squirrel in a tree!" The crowd went nuts with laughter and the women jumped away from Karen closing her robe."

"Are you okay now, Karen?" Jeff asked with concern, and not finding much humor in the accident; more interested in Karen's health condition.

"Yes I'm fine except for humiliation and a lump on my head. The store manager gave me my choice of any dress that I wanted, so I got a free dress."

When the dinner was over and the group was having dessert, Joan noticed Jeff was more interested in what was happening at the bar than sharing the interests at the table. Joan wanted to quit analyzing, but found that something was telling her she was close to solving Jeff's problem. Jeff got up from the table, excused himself, and walked over to the bar. The group observed his odd behavior, but didn't say a word. They got up and headed for the elevator. The door was closing when Jeff stopped it and stepped in. "I thought you were going to have a drink at the bar," remarked Alice.

"No I just wanted to ask that couple at the bar a question." Joan with a frown asked, "Did you know them?"

"No." When they got to the sixth floor, it was decided in the elevator that they were all going out on the town. Jeff declined with the excuse that he would be writing his acceptance speech this evening. Joan stared at Jeff for a minute, knowing full well that something changed him, suddenly. He was fine while having dinner, then he reversed his mood in the elevator. That triggered something in her mind.

CHAPTER 8

Spinga and Mark left the elevator with the excitement of two kids. Their legs couldn't take long enough strides getting to Jeff's room as if they were running with kangaroos. Spinga started pounding on the door and shouting for Jeff to open up. It took Jeff more than a minute to open the door, but finally when he did, they also woke everyone down the hallway including all the other hotel guests.

"What is it with you guys?" demanded Alice. "You two scared everyone on this floor." Mark looked down the hall and smiled sheepishly. "We're sorry, we'll keep it down." The two crowded around Jeff trying to escape the death stares, and snuck into his room. The ladies followed right behind them with the hopes of finding out what all the excitement was about. They all sat around Jeff's bed waiting intently for the news. Jeff sat down at the table wondering if it was a mistake to have brought this cast of characters.

Spinga began, "We were down in the lobby a few minutes ago, snooping. Did you guys know Governor Rudy Giuliani is coming to Jeff's Award Banquet?" All the heads turned to Jeff who said, "To begin with, Rudy is the Mayor, not the Governor."

"Who cares," responded Mark, "He's bigger than any Governor."

"Rudy is a friend of mine. I've known him from back when he was a federal prosecutor."

Spinga jumped off the bed. "Listen gang, Mark and I saw the list of V.I.P. guests and it is full of actors, producers, and big shots from this whole city."

"We'll be lucky just to get in the room, let alone find a seat anywhere," chided Mark.

Jeff smiled, "You guys will be sitting at the front table in the center." Spinga shouted to Mark, "Wow, we're big shots tonight!" Jeff rolled his eyes then asked everyone to please leave so he could try and prepare his speech.

At five-thirty p.m. two security men came to the rooms to escort Jeff's entourage to the center table of the dining room. Jeremy Sutton came to Jeff's open door, and knocked lightly. "Come in Jeremy, I want to speak with you for a second." "We don't have a lot of time, Jeff." The two sat down. Jeff reached for his notes and showed Jeremy. "You see what I have written down?"

"Your speech has one line. That's all you have written?"

"No Jeremy, I didn't even write that. My neighbor wrote this to motivate me to, maybe, write something provocative. I have no speech." Jeff began to pull for air. Jeremy bowed his head for a moment, then tapped Jeff on the shoulder, "I don't want you having a heart attack while doing something you have no interest in doing. I'll introduce you, then I'll say some words on your behalf. How does that sound?"

Jeff took a couple deep breaths, nearly hyperventilating, then smiled, "You're such a good friend, Jeremy. But if it wasn't for you, I wouldn't have attended this awards thing." Moments later the two entered the dining hall. Everyone stood to applaud with thunderous appreciation. When the two got to the front Jeff stopped at the center table. Josh was standing and applauding his dad. Jeff came over to Josh and gave him a hug and sat down. "What made you come?" I thought you were snowed under with school work?"

"No dad, this is far more important than anything in my life. I'm here for you, dad."

The waiter brought Josh a chair, moving everyone over slightly, then the servers began with spinach and sweet butter lettuce salad to Jeff's table first, then on around the room. Jeff nibbled some on the salad, but his worry about what he was going to say over powered his need for food. When they brought the main course of Chicken Devan, Jeff just pushed it around, never putting any in his mouth. Jeremy kept glancing at Jeff, wondering what he could say to relax him..." I'll go up there and throw a few words around so it'll break the ice for you." Joan felt so sorry for Jeff, knowing full well that if she had not planted the seed for him to change his life style, he would never have considered this trip.

When the dessert, lemon tart with fresh whipped cream was served, Jeff's stomach went into near up-chuck. Jeremy looked over the room, with everyone finishing their dessert.

Jeremy started to break away to head up to the podium. Jeff stopped him and whispered, I'm going to do it." "I'm with you all the way Jeff because I know you can do this." Jeff gave Jeremy a slightly harder tap on his back than average, and climbed the three steps to the podium and gazed out into the vast number of friends and colleagues. Jeff put his hand over his eyes to lessen the glaring lights. The hotel manager quickly ordered the lights dimmed.

Jeff raised his hand to stop the applause. Almost instantly the house became quiet. Jeff looked down at Josh and his dear neighbors, then ran his eyes across the room before uttering a word. He began to smile, as if words were coming to mind. He was ready:

"My wife Marilyn, whom I lost to cancer three years ago, always said, 'I will write children's books for the young and when they get old enough they'll start on yours.' We were a team. Marilyn and I had two children, Jodie whom we lost in a bus accident when she was six, now it's just Josh and me. My hope is that Josh will find someone like his mother to share his life with." The crowd smiled and sensed the deep emotional stress he was fighting, but also sensed something was coming that would be very personable.

"As a lot of you know, I have been working on my latest novel dedicated to my wife, Marilyn, without much success, I might add. This novel reminds me of a fighter, a boxer, who wants to fight longer, but doesn't have the legs nor the heart to continue. In all likelihood, this will be my last book." The whispers were sounding throughout the hall.

"I'm not much for these kinds of functions. Marilyn and I both felt that awards were totally unnecessary. We both felt that the acceptance of our work was reward enough. To change someone's life because they read your book, is the greatest thing life can give a writer. I have always written for the good of man, not to instill some kind of ideology in another, but to give people a genuine caring love... I thank you all for the many loving years you have given me. Thank you.

There was dead silence in the dining hall. Jeremy Sutton hustled up to the podium to break the sadness and give the award. "Ladies and gentlemen, with all the admiration and pleasure I possess, I give the Literary Lifetime Award for the Decade to Jeffrey Williams, even if he never writes again He will be remembered for generations to come." A thunderous applause reverberated throughout the room and all the way to the bar.

The congratulatory handshakes seemed never ending. When the dinner awards banquet concluded and most had gone out the door, his table was still intact. Joan leaned over and grabbed Jeff's hand with a grin, "I thought you gave a great impromptu speech."

"Hey dad, does Joan realize that you can read her emotions when you hold her hand?" Joan turned red faced and let go. "Josh, how do you know that I can't read your dad's the same way?"

"Whoa dad, is Joan telling me that both of you are telepathic?"

"We are just having fun tonight, son." They all got up from the table and filed out to the elevator. "Well dad, congratulations on that great award even though you may not think it's necessary... Well, I must get back to school."

"Why don't you stay the night and go home with us tomorrow? You can stay in my room."

"Cheryl is over there at the door waiting for me. A couple of my friends are waiting in the car out front."

"Why don't you invite all of them to join us upstairs?"

"Listen dad... Cheryl will not even come over here to say hello, let alone go upstairs." Jeff gave his son a hug then Josh said his goodbyes to the group. Mark could see how much it hurt Jeff, not to have a good relationship with Josh's girlfriend.

Everyone was silent in the elevator up to the sixth floor. When the doors opened Alice gave Jeff a hug. "I have an idea. Why don't you and Joan go to Central Park tomorrow morning to visit places you and Marilyn use to enjoy? Something may trigger your mind and send you back to writing.... I'm sorry to hear you say, 'writing is over for you,'" Jeff, gave a shoulder shrug to Joan, meaning it was no big thing. "I'll be ready at 9 a.m. if you want to go, Jeff."

"Okay."

The two were out the hotel door and in a taxi before 9 a.m. "Central Park, please," shouted Jeff. The traffic was light on this Sunday morning going to the park, saving them time before having to get back to the hotel and head home.

Joan could see that Jeff was in his element. His personality lit up like the Rockefeller Christmas Tree. The two walked almost tirelessly on walking paths, exploring the exquisite beauty of the park. Joan knew they were close to that park bench that Jeff so fondly recalled in times past between him and Marilyn. Even with her heavy overcoat, she could feel Jeff's arm clutching around her waist giving a gentle nudge to go faster.

From a distance she could see the very bench that was so dear to his memory. The kid's play ground, the foot path bridge that was filmed probably in more movies than anything else in Central Park. When they got to the bench, Jeff, with a sober face, asked, "Would you like to sit?"

"I would love to, Mr. Williams from Rutgers." Jeff was caught off guard with that response. It was a reply that Marilyn would have said. The two sat down, nestled tightly against the morning chill. Jeff watched the kid's swinging and his eyes began to tear. "Tell me Jeff, what you are feeling. I am still playing the part of psychologist first. Jeff smiled as though he was game to play the subject.

"We would sit here, and Marilyn would observe what the kids were doing. She would see things that I would never see in a hundred years. It was amazing how she would come away from here and have a full story that kids and adults could relate to. She was so much better in her writing than me in mine. Joan raised her gloved hand to Jeff's face and asked, "May I kiss you Jeff? We have never really kissed and I need to."

"That's funny Joan, because it feels like we have kissed hundreds of times."

"I could learn to hate you, Jeffrey Williams. You always seem to be one step ahead of me all the time."

"You want me to kiss you in front of all these children, Doctor Steele?"

"Yes, Jeffrey Williams, in front of all these kids, because… he begins to kiss and kiss and kiss. It was like he was releasing all his emotions that were trapped inside of him. A five-year-old boy pulled on Jeff's jacket for his attention. The two turned to the boy. "My mother said, (pointing to her) that you grownups should not be kissing in the park." Joan looked at Jeff then back to the boy. "Tell her she should try it sometime?"

"Eeew, no way, my mommy only kisses me." The two got up and began their walk toward the street to hail a cab. "Joan, you said the word 'because' before we kissed, as though it would not happen after "because of something." Joan didn't know how to tell him. With just a few more steps to the street, she fell silent for a second, but her professionalism took over. "Jeff, when I told you that I am one of the best psychologist in the world, I was not bragging. It pains me, no end, to tell you this theory of mine, and it is just a theory, so if you don't want me to say anything about your book problem, tell me now."

"Here is our cab. Tell me in the cab." The cab just left the curb when Joan began her analysis: "If I'm way off base on this, please tell me to shut-up and it's done and forgotten. Everything that I read by listening to you, tells me your marriage had an affair." Jeff didn't stop her from speaking, so she went on. "At first I thought it was that you'd had an affair, but then I heard you defending Marilyn constantly, which threw the affair over to Marilyn. I also think it happened in the hotel we're staying in. Last night the couple at the bar, total strangers, were of interest to you. Why? Because you thought they were going to have an affair." Tears were streaming down Jeff's face, uncontrollably. His hands were trembling. His face had lost its color. Joan reached to hold his hand. He snapped his away.

"There is a little more, but I won't say anymore if you don't want me to." Jeff turned his head toward the window and never looked at Joan the rest of the way to the hotel and all the way back to Litchfield. No one remarked about the change in how Jeff and Joan were acting. They left the two alone, talking amongst themselves.

CHAPTER 9

The packing was nearly complete when the phone rang. Jeff hurriedly sidestepped three suitcases already packed, nearly tripping. "Hello, hello!" "Hi Jeff, this is Alice, can I come over and speak to you, or is this a bad time?"

"Alice, how long have we known each other? Twenty years or more and you still don't think I recognize your voice?"

"It's a habit, Jeff. So, can I come over?"

"Sure."

Alice entered the back door and saw the packed bags lined up down the hallway. Alice shouted, "Jeff, I'm here." Jeff sounded, "I'm in the bedroom." She walked in and sat on the edge of the bed and watched Jeff cram a pair of shoes into an already full suitcase.

"How long are you planning to stay in Missoula? The way you've packed, I would say a long time."

"Long enough to complete this book, then maybe I can go fishing in my retirement.

"You don't know how to fish, and besides your impatience wouldn't allow the line to be in the water more than five seconds. Do you realize how much bait you would lose? It would break you just in the cost of bait." They both started to laugh, with

Alice breaking into a much needed cry. Jeff zipped the last piece of luggage and sat next to her on the bed.

"Alice stop the crying. It's time everyone just let me be and let me solve my own problems. Everyone around here has to be sick of my moaning and groaning about this book. It is up to me to get out of the doldrums and start moving forward. Don't feel sorry for me anymore. Would you do that, Alice?"

She hugged Jeff for the longest time and finally agreed.

"Well I'm packed, so now I wait for Josh to call and tell me when he's close to New Haven. He and his girlfriend are planning to have lunch with me, and maybe I can make his girlfriend like me, even if it's just a little.

"Do you have to leave today? Why don't you leave after Thanksgiving?"

"Thanksgiving is a week away, and I know what you're going to say, I'm just too impetuous."

"That's exactly what you are. To think you'll be all alone at Thanksgiving when you could be enjoying yourself around all your friends."

"Things may turn around for me on this trip, but if it doesn't; so be it. It's time for me to get over it and move on."

"Okay, Jeff, I've said all I'm going to say. I'm not going to cry for you anymore, but try and make this a short trip. I miss you already and you haven't even left yet."

"I don't think I'll be gone that long, two or three weeks max. The drive to and from Montana will take about half the time. If it's longer than a month it means I have a problem, and this trip that Joan suggested I take, will be for naught."

"Speaking of Joan; can't you bring yourself to go over to her house and talk out whatever is bugging you?"

"Why is it, Alice, that you keep trying to push us together?"

"She is perfect for you. She see's things in you that I have never seen."

"What? You guys have been talking private things about me?"

"Give her a chance."

"She's not marrying material. Every time we were apart, I'd wonder if she was cheating on me. She's been married four times, that is not a good track record."

"You are so wrong… She was used, big time, by those four losers… Did you know that her I.Q. is at genius levels? Did you also know that she gave her last husband, the philanderer, a generous settlement of a million dollars so he could live his lavish, playboy life style. She could not handle his cheating ways. That's why she found you so unique and above anyone she has ever known."

"You're doing it again, Alice. You're pushing Joan on me."

"Your right, Jeff. I won't do it anymore, but will you go say goodbye to her when you decide to leave, right? Or maybe even, right now?" Jeff just closed his eyes hoping Alice would leave and she did.

Jeff paced the floor wondering how he would say goodbye to Joan, just to satisfy Alice's persistence. He felt anger, disappointment and even resentment for her. But was it really a dislike, or was it that she was right and it was tough facing the truth? Jeff sat in his big chair in the living room wishing the phone would ring and he'd be off to New Haven for lunch, but that didn't happen. Instead he picked up the phone and called Joan. With three rings, his mind told him she was out and it was time to hang up. After all, he tried; then she answered, catching Jeff stuttering to say hello.

"Is that you Jeff? I can't distinguish your voice with so many H's in hello."

"Yes it's me. Alice felt I should say goodbye."

"Okay, goodbye." Jeff stood holding the phone with nobody on the other end. He dropped the phone, leaving it hanging and began to mumble to himself, as he walked out the door and headed to Joan's house. (Boy, if this is the way geniuses think, maybe a new standard of smarts should be tried.) He tapped on her door lightly. She quickly opened the door. "Yes?"

"Oh! Were you going out? You answered the door rather quickly… the phone disconnected. I didn't hang up on you."

"No, I hung up on you because Alice had suggested you say goodbye and you said it, so that was sufficient." She started to close the door, then Jeff stuck his arm to hold it open.

"Oh, I just thought we should talk a little."

"Well, you have already spoken a little, so isn't that enough for you?"

"I need to talk more."

"Then maybe you should come in before you freeze to death." He took off his parka and scarf, placing it on the foyer table. She pointed to the living room couch to sit, not saying a word. Jeff sat on the couch thinking she would sit next to him to talk, but she didn't.

"It sure is cozy in here compared to my house."

"All you have to do is turn up your heat to get the same results." She was not reacting like he had hoped. He took a deep breath, trying to find the right words to break through her frigid feelings. "I want to apologize for my behavior in New York." She interrupts. "No Jeff, I had no right sounding off with my opinions when I didn't have a complete study on you." Jeff slid forward to the edge of the couch. "Do you think I could sit closer to you? Ten feet seems a far distance for me." She tapped a spot on the couch next to her and he quickly shifted to her couch. Jeff was ready to reveal his story and put it behind him. "Alice said you are something special and I should appreciate how difficult life has been for you. I'm sorry for the way I acted. So I have decided, just now, to tell you the whole story."

"I don't really want to hear about you and Marilyn."

"Please, Joan, I owe you the full truth."

"If it makes you feel better, and it puts this torment behind you, then go ahead." Jeff sighed, he looked at the gentle flame in the fireplace and began: "Marilyn and I did a lot of traveling to the publishers and editors over the years, together and apart. It was between Thanksgiving and Christmas; Marilyn was getting pressure from her publisher to complete her latest book. She writes, if you have ever read her books, about animals that represent people and their families. Readers have grown to love how Marilyn, incorporated animals to represent people in her stories. It adds humor to their serious family misfortunes. This was why she had a fenced back yard with a hundred animals. It cost us a small fortune to feed them. I was already in London introducing my new book, when this affair happened. Yes, you were right, it was an affair."

"You said, at first, you thought I was the one that had an affair, but then realized it was Marilyn. Yes, it was Marilyn. It was in the Roosevelt Hotel. The same one that all of us stayed in. She and he had a drink and went to his room. You were so right that it was spooky. It seemed like you saw the whole affair in your analysis." Joan reached for Jeff's hand and this time he clutched hers.

"… It was Sam, my best friend, Alice's husband, my golfing buddy, the great foursome that we were." Joan slung her arms around him and just held on tight. The two didn't say a word. She knew the horrible pain that he had carried for years. He pulled back to continue.

"It was ten days after the affair that I returned from Europe. Sam was a wreck every time he saw me. Marilyn seldom looked me straight in the eyes. When Sam showed no interest in playing golf and just sat around the house doing nothing instead, I began to fear something had happened between Sam and Marilyn."

"How was it that they were both in New York at the same time?"

"That's a good question, Joan... Sam, who does job placements for college grads, was participating in the convention at the Roosevelt and Marilyn was taking a seminar on writing kids' books. The two ended up at the bar later. Being away from home, having a few drinks, and feeling lonely, they foolishly had a one-night stand."

"A few weeks later I was out jogging, with near frozen lungs, and anxious to get home. When I came in the back door and through the kitchen I could see Marilyn standing at the doorway to the writing room crying. I asked what was wrong, and then I saw Sam sitting on the couch. The first thing I thought was Alice had an accident and died. Sam jumped to his feet. 'Can you ever forgive me Jeff? I had an affair with Marilyn.' I looked over at Marilyn and saw a person totally broken... Go home Sam and don't tell Alice about this, it'll crush her."'

I told Marilyn that we must close this chapter and go on. She put the crucifix above the writing room door and became a church goer from then on. I went with her, occasionally. Sam and I went back to golfing to keep Alice from asking why he wasn't going anymore. Sam and I became friends again, but with guarded feelings." Jeff's cell phone rang. It was Josh, ready to meet his dad in two hours. Jeff got up to leave. Joan went to the foyer and handed him his parka and scarf. "Is there anything I can say to keep you from going to Missoula?" Joan asked.

Jeff responded, "No, you were exactly right when you said I had to go."

"I am so sorry that I said those words." The two hugged, holding each other's warmth, then Joan whispered as though somebody was listening. "May I go in your house and read all the books that you and Marilyn have written?"

"Why don't you just bring them home and read them?"

"Because I want to read them where they were written. I have these vibes you know, just like the man who holds me does... Please call us when you get there so we know you made it safely." Jeff gave her his house key, even though Alice had one; plus, he'd probably forget to lockup anyway.

Jeff walked back to his house feeling relieved that Joan knew the whole story. He could hear the dial tone when he entered. He smiled, seeing the phone receiver just hanging by its cord as though it belonged that way. He placed it back on the holder then looked around all the rooms to say goodbye to his home. His last stop was the writing room. "Well Marilyn, I'm saying goodbye to you here, but I'll be saying hello to you in Missoula. That seems strange, doesn't it?"

He threw his bags in his Jag and headed out to meet up with Josh for lunch, and then to begin his nineteen- hundred-mile journey.

CHAPTER 10

The trip to Missoula took two and a half days, a little longer than planned because of a stop at a jewelry store in Chicago. Jeff arrived in Missoula with a feeling he never wanted to sit in his Jag ever again. His beautiful dark blue Jag had gone through every type of weather imaginable, leaving it looking junky. Jeff pulled off the interstate to study his map for the proximity of the school and Marilyn's home where she grew up. He would be very close at the next exit. He looked at his face in the rearview mirror to see if he was presentable before he left the car to check in a hotel. "Yikes, you look like hell, but at this late hour, maybe the lobby will be empty." He seemed to be talking to himself a lot on this trip.

Having only visited Missoula a few times and being unfamiliar with the area, had given him second thoughts about making this trip. He told himself repeatedly how stupid he was to make this trip, and that he should just turn around and go home, but he couldn't.

It was almost eight p.m. when he made a left turn onto Broadway. "Yes, yes, I remember a hotel close by." After driving two blocks down East Broadway, he knew he was close, but couldn't think of the hotel name. When he saw the Holiday Inn, he smiled, "Of course it was the Holiday" and pulled in. He checked in with a request for the top floor, the fourth. He wanted a room that was high enough to study the lay of the town. He got to his room, dropped his luggage near the bed and called Alice. She didn't answer so he left a message on her recorder to call Josh and Joan that he was in Missoula. He felt far too tired to call anybody else. A shower was all he was thinking about.

After a restless night of sleeping, yet still mentally driving, Jeff woke with a weary mind, but was ready to search out a storyline that would give him some writing material. He dressed in a suit, a tie and a heavy overcoat.

A thin layer of snow lay on the ground from the night before. He left the hotel and drove to the cemetery to visit Marilyn and Jodie. The snow dusted both tombstones. Jeff softly cleaned them, laboring to hold back tears. A burst of emotions overcame his resolve. A few minutes would help him regain his composure. He knelt between the markers and said a prayer of thanks that he was here with them.

... "I'm here, Marilyn to finish the book about you. Jodie, maybe you could help along the way. Between you and your mother, finishing this book should be easy. So Jodie, start building sentences for me... I would give up my life today to get to spend one moment with you two. But if God won't allow that, then let me feel your spirit." He dropped his head in tears. When he raised his head, a quiet calm came over him as he said his goodbyes, giving each headstone a kiss.

Driving his filthy car out of the cemetery, it took him to West Beckwith Street, a quiet area of older homes and longtime residents. The homes were all very similar to an unfamiliar eye as Jeff drove down the street a few times trying to recall his bearings from the distant past. He stopped in front of the house that seemed to give him the most nostalgia. A few minutes went by. He was reluctant to go to the front door and invade the lives of these people. Disgusted, he forced himself to leave the car. Leaning up against the driver's side he visualizes Marilyn coming out the front door, with bony legs, lanky height, and her beautiful hazel green eyes. She would look down the street for her friends to accompany her to school. Maybe a few more friends joined them on the way to school, he thinks....

Jeff's thoughts were interrupted when a car entered the driveway. His eyes followed the man as he left the car and came over to him. "Excuse me sir, can I help you?" He hesitated. "My name is Jeffrey Williams and I..."

"The writer, the one that was married to Marilyn Dunne?" Jeff was shocked at the response, and uttered, "yes!"

"I have read most of your books. My daughters grew up reading Ms. Dunne's. When we bought this house, word all over town was, 'You were the ones who bought Marilyn Dunne's house'. So what brings you to Missoula?"

"This may sound foolish to you, but I'm writing a novel about Marilyn and I'm having a great deal of trouble completing it. I thought maybe if I came to her hometown, found out where her grammar school and the University of Montana up on the hill was, I'd get some kind of inspiration... I better get going."

"I'm home for a few minutes for lunch, then I have to get back to work, otherwise I would invite you in. If you go down to the end of the street and turn left it will take you to her grammar school and then continue on and you'll be at the college... I'm a lawyer. I do work for the city and I have my own practice called 'Bill Maxwell Law Offices.' My whole family has read both yours and your wife's books. You staying in town?"

"I'm staying at the Holiday. I'll only be here for a few days." The two shook hands and said their goodbyes. Jeff drove down to the end of the block and began his visions of how Marilyn would look as she walked with her friends to school. Her every step was imprinting Jeff's mind. At times he would stop, close his eyes and try to see this tall, skinny kid growing through the years, laughing and enjoying her friends. It wasn't coming through. With only an hour of daylight remaining, Jeff drove to University Avenue, on the University of Montana campus. When he got to Arthur Avenue, he parked and left the car. He exited the car to look for… what? He was trolling for ghosts of Marilyn's past. First he briefly walked north, but nothing stirred in him, so he crossed at the intersection and moved west. But frustrated with no answers or impressions, he turned to the east for quite some distance… nothing. That failing, he continued to look around as he slowly moved south and back to the beginning. When he got back to the car, he leaned up against it, then whispered with his eyes closed, "Come on Marilyn help me out. Give me the feel I'm looking for, please."

His erratic behavior drew looks from a few inquisitive students. When Jeff opened his eyes, he could only stare in disbelief. "You kids are looking at me as though I'm crazy." A girl took a step forward and asked, "It does look like you have lost your bearings. Can we help you?"

"I don't think anyone can help me. I've had two shrinks trying to solve my problem with no luck. The students registered the word *shrink*, and decided to let the old man work out his own problems. One student couldn't resist a passing remark before he got out of earshot and yelled back, "With a car like that, you could at least keep it clean! What a disgrace!" He took a quick step towards the kids, causing them to scramble backward.

Wishing for more daylight, he reluctantly drove back to the hotel to make a feeble attempt at writing.

Bill Maxwell was on his drive home from the office and could not believe having visited with Jeffrey Williams at lunch. The girls are going to be excited to hear about what we talked about, he thought. 'Yes, your dear old dad spoke to the man who married the very woman who lived in our house. The girls won't be ignoring me so they can talk on the phone, or have any excuses to do more important things than to speak with dear old dad. Hmmm...maybe I'll wait and tell them after supper'. His day dreaming stopped when he pulled into the driveway and drove to the back garage. He picked up his brief case from the seat, not realizing the case was unlatched, resulting papers strewn all across the front seat. Frustrated, he gathered them quickly, trying to ignore the icy temperature in the garage. He closed the garage door and ran to the first step looking up at the landing to the back door. He saw his younger daughter standing at the top, she stood with her arms folded, matching the upset look on her face. "Keeley, what are you doing standing outside? It's got to be 32 degrees out here... and where's your jacket?"

"Where's Mr. Williams? Is he coming in a few minutes?"

"Come on Keeley, let's get out of this cold air before you get sick and miss Thanksgiving". She walked backwards to the door wanting an explanation.

"Please, Keeley, let me get in the door and give me a chance to relax a little. I was hoping I could tell you girls about Mr. Williams, after dinner." He turned her around and they both went in.

"After dinner? Why can't you tell me now? I know it's bad news, because you didn't bring him home with you." Bill glared at his wife Lauren because she was clearly to blame for having told the girls about Jeff.

"Your mother just had to tell the both of you, before I got home, didn't she! Look Keeley, your sister is calm about all of this, she's even helping your mother set the table like a good daughter and not badgering her dad."

"Tracy is 21 years old and a college graduate. She should be out of the house. She has a boyfriend and everything. She doesn't care about great writers.

Well, I'm sorry Keeley for not thinking straight, but you are out of line."

"I'm sorry too, dad, but you know I want to be a writer more than anything in this world... I sort of apologize, but you should have thought about my feelings."

"You should apologize to Tracy for that thoughtless remark." Keeley looked at her mother then back to her dad, wishing they'd forget about all this apologizing stuff. "Okay, umm, I apologize, Tracy, but you all should know that I... will be gone from this house when I turn eighteen.

Her dad smiled then tried to hold back his chuckle, "Well young lady, how do you plan on paying for college?" Keeley answered quickly, "Well, I haven't gotten that far, but I have some ideas."

The next morning Bill was heading to work but changed directions and drove to the Holiday Inn Hotel. He saw the dirty Jag parked near the admittance office. He was relieved that Mr. Williams was still here. Bill parked next to the Jag and entered the side door to the office.

"Hello, is anyone here?" A man came out from a back room, yawning and looking as though the night had gotten the better of him. "May I help you sir?" Another yawn and a distorted facial expression, was all it took to make Bill pop a yawn too. "Would you call Jeff Williams' room and ask him if I might see him. My name is Bill Maxwell.

"Yes I can call him, but I can't give you his room number."

"I know the rules for your guests." The clerk dialed the number and waited for the fourth ring then hung up. "He doesn't answer."

"Could you try it once more and maybe let it ring ten times? It's an emergency."

"Everybody has an emergency these days," yawned the man as he redialed, letting it ring longer this time. A hello came from the other end. "Boy, Mr. Williams, you sound sleepier than I do. A Mr. Maxwell is here and he would like an audience with you." Send him up was the reply. "You may go up to room 406."

"An audience?"

"Yeah, I heard that word on the news when some big shot politician was in Rome at the Vatican.

Jeff heard the soft knock on the door and gave a yell, "Come on in!" Maxwell came in and was shocked by all the paper wads scattered around the table where Jeff was attempting to write.

"You write on legal pad paper? I thought writers wrote on a computer or typewriters."

"Mr. Maxwell, I normally do, but this book about Marilyn is making me a little crazy. If I were to use a typewriter, I'd be throwing it out the window every hour, and that is not cost effective. Paper is the way to go… Now I don't want to be rude Mr. Maxwell, but I have not slept all night and I sure would like to try and get some sleep."

"I'll make this quick Mr. Williams."

"Please, no more Mister. Call me Jeff or call me Williams.

"Okay and please call me Bill."

"Okay Mr. Maxwell I will." Bill did a double take when he heard Jeff's response.

"Our family would like you to come over tomorrow for Thanksgiving."

"I can't intrude in your lives. No sir, I can't do that"

"Please Jeff, my daughter Keeley will never forgive me if you don't… I'll show you the whole house. I'll show you Marilyn's room." That brought attention and sadness to his mind. Shaking the sadness off he quickly reverted to humor. "You're serving turkey and ham?"

"If you don't want ham, we absolutely will not have it."

"I'm only kidding with you Mr. Maxwell, I'm not Jewish… I'll start calling you Bill tomorrow, Mr. Maxwell."

"Do you want to come over about eleven-thirty? We usually go to Mass at St. Anthony's Catholic Church at ten o'clock."

"Yes, I'm going to Mass myself. I didn't know the time of the service, so thanks."

"Wait a minute, how about we come over here, pick you up at nine-forty-five and we'll all go in my car?"

"Will that be ok with your wife?"

"Lauren would love to have you go."

"Okay I'll be ready. Good day Mr. Maxwell I really have to get some sleep. I've been up all night"

"Good day, sir. We will give you a warm Missoula welcome.

CHAPTER 11

Thanksgiving

This was going to be the greatest surprise of Keeley's young life. Her mother and father promised that going to church on this day would be a wonderful experience for her. She just frowned and shrugged, accepting what was forced on her. She was always reluctant to attend mass, especially one that is not a holy day of obligation, much to the chagrin of her parents. Her words were, "If God is everywhere, then he will hear my words in my room." Lauren opened the oven door, introducing a wonderful fragrance to the whole house. She checked the temperature of the two birds, then turned down the oven temperature to 200 degrees hoping the birds would be done when they returned from church.

Bill backed the car out of the garage and up to the back door. He could hear Keeley complaining as she came down the back door steps, "It's silly to leave at nine-thirty, when it only takes ten minutes to church." Tracy, knowing the secret, demanded she stop her complaining, "You know that *Father knows best.*"

Keeley still resisting said, "Just because you grew up with the *Father Knows Best* family, doesn't mean I did. I wasn't even born when that show was on T.V. or even the reruns." Dad gave both of them stern looks in the rear view mirror and shouted, "Buckle up!"

"Well Dad, I can see why you're upset with Tracy, but not with me. After all, you were the one who unwittingly didn't act like a kind father." They gave up arguing with Keeley, knowing she always had more words to say in her arguments.

Bill backed out of the driveway and onto the street. With more snow on the ground from the night before, it was good that he had changed to snow cleated tires for the winter. Today Bill's route to the church was different. He veered from it to head to the Holiday Inn. When he turned and took a right into the Inn's parking lot, Keeley leaned forward, "Okay dad, I am only thirteen. Dad, I said when I turn eighteen I'd be ready to leave home." Lauren turned to Bill, "Is that him in the lobby?"

"Yes."

"He sure dresses well. Maybe someone else could take lessons." Jeff exited the motel and walked up to the car. Keeley knew, from the photographs on the back of his books, who Jeff Williams was. She froze when he opened her door. "Move over, Honey, so Mr. Williams can sit down." Lauren introduced herself, then the girls. Keeley sat with her hands clasped tightly on her knees, looking at her father then to her mother, but never at Mr. Williams directly.

When the five arrived at St. Anthony's, Keeley was beaming and looking for her friends. It was a little early; so most would come in just before Mass began. Keeley stayed back with her father as the other three entered the door. "Thanks dad, I love you. I didn't mean what I said about leaving home the minute I turn eighteen. Once in a while I speak too quickly."

"I know Keeley. That's most of the time, but I wouldn't have it any other way." Bill waited in the back getting the collection baskets set up for Mass. Keeley hurried up to the front to make sure the seating arrangement was to her satisfaction. She waited for sister Tracy to enter the pew first, then mother Lauren, then she slipped in signaling Mr. Williams to follow her. They knelt to say their prayers, except Mr. Williams, he sat down. Keeley, with her head down saying her prayers, moved her eyes to him without moving her head.

She sat down after her short, very short, prayer, and whispered to Mr. Williams, "Just watch me when I stand and sit. I come to church all the time, so I know what I'm doing. We do a lot of standing, sitting, and kneeling. It can be tricky if you don't know what you're doing."

"Thank you for the help, Keeley." She looked over to her mother and sister with a smile as though she we're handling the situation. Her eyes glanced farther across the aisle where she could see several of her friends gesturing to her about who was sitting next to her. She gave that knowing grin that was her trademark, when she was thrilled.

Her friends swarmed her after Mass, wanting an explanation about who was sitting next to her. When she called Mr. Williams to them and introduced him, the girls couldn't believe who they were seeing. It was so surreal to them; that this had to be a miracle. All they ever heard was that Marilyn Dunne had grown up in Keeley's house and had been a real published author married to Jeffrey Williams, an even bigger name than his wife.

The girls were all in the same school writing group as Keeley, and all dreamed of becoming writers, much because of Keeley's worshipful fanaticism about Marilyn.

The Maxwells and Jeff walked to their car with the girls in hot pursuit, following while trying to find pen and paper in their purses, for his autograph. Bill turned to the girls, "I'm sorry girls, but Mr. Williams is our guest for Thanksgiving and he doesn't want to be pressured." The girls looked at Jeff and then to Keeley, hoping for some kind of acceptance. "I have an idea Dad. Why can't my writing group come over after we have dinner and speak with Mr. Williams?"

"Keeley, Mr. Williams probably wants to rest at his hotel and write."

"Not really, Bill. I'm here to find out how Marilyn lived and the things she did growing up. If these girls can give me some insight, I'd appreciate it a great deal." They all turned their heads back to Bill, even Lauren and Tracy. "Okay, but when Mr. Williams gets tired and weary of your questions, you kids will have to leave. Understood?" They all agreed to the terms and then one asked, "What time?" Lauren, with a stern voice, "not earlier than three."

On the way back to the house, Jeff began to interview each family member. He felt very relaxed with his new friends, "So how long have you guys lived in your home?" Bill and Lauren looked at each other realizing that the home was an important part of his trip to Missoula.

Lauren turned half way around to face Jeff, "We bought the home after Marilyn's father died." Jeff was running numbers in his head figuring out how long the family lived in Marilyn's house. Lauren smiled, "Keeley wasn't yet born, so it's been more than thirteen years now. You didn't come to Mr. Dunne's funeral?"

"No, I was in France doing some research for a book I was working on." Keeley's eyes lit up hearing Jeff say he traveled to a foreign country for information on his book. How glamorous is that? She thought. Jeff turned his interest to Tracy. "Are you still in school?"

"I'm studying to be a Veterinarian at the college here. My uncle, Dad's brother, has a large cattle ranch northwest of town and I'm planning on taking care of his herd, along with a small animal clinic here in town."

"My Son, Josh, is studying Veterinary and Biological Science as a graduate student at University of Connecticut. What drove him to that field was strictly coincidental... I was driving down to Waterbury, Connecticut, with Marilyn and Josh, when we saw a cow lying flat, on its side near the fence in a pasture. We saw this man parked ahead of us running around his pickup looking for something."

"Was he looking for a knife?"

"Yes, that's exactly what he was looking for. How did you know?"

"It must have been spring time when all the grasses are tender. The cow was probably bloated"

"Bingo. You hit it right on the head.... Maybe, he could come out here and meet you?"

"Please Mr. Williams, don't be a match maker like my parents. They never seem to appreciate anyone I like." Bill and Lauren ignored her remarks by making small talk between them.

"My son Josh doesn't seem to know how to pick a great girl. I can give you his phone number and maybe you two can meet."

"Mr. Williams, I'm betting he would be climbing the walls if he heard you talk this way. You sound a lot like my parents." Lauren shouts to change the subject, "We're home!" Leaving the car Keeley hurried to follow, almost grabbing his coat jacket, "Mr. Williams, would you like to go with Dad and me to the mission?" The minute Lauren entered the house she pulled the turkeys from the oven, "They're done, and ready for you guy's to take one.

"Sure I would love to go."

"Mom cooks two turkeys for Thanksgiving and, two at Christmas, then we take one to the mission for the homeless... We're going now."

"I would love to go." Bill brought out the great smelling turkey, on a covered platter, Jeff opened the hatchback door, allowing Bill to lay the platter on the car floor. "Let's go," declared Bill as if he'd cooked the turkey himself and was preparing to get a lot of praise at the mission.

When they arrived, Jeff could see a sizable group going into the hall. A giant black man was telling everyone coming through the door, where to sit. Jeff followed Bill and Keeley to the door. The huge man wanted to talk to Bill about something. The eighteen-pound turkey was starting to feel more like forty, to Bill. "I hope you can do something about the school situation, Bill."

"I'll look into it, Jacob, but if I don't get this bird on the table, my arms are going to be permanently locked in this position. Jacob pointed where he wanted the bird, then he stopped Keeley, "So young lady, how is school treating you?"

"I'm not learning fast enough." Jacob smiled as though he knew what she was going to say. She moved forward so Jeff could enter. Jacob stuck out his size 24xx hand and with a raised voice said, "Now who are you?"

Jeff with a knot in his throat looked up at this giant who is at least a foot and a half taller declared, "I'm with Keeley and Bill and I'm not going to be eating." Jacob broke into a gentle smile, "I'm Jacob Staley, they call me the Black Giant, I run this place."

"I'm Jeff Williams. I'm staying here for a week or so."

Jacob asked, "You're Jeffrey Williams, the writer?"

"Yes."

Keeley could see Jacob's eyes light up and she did not like what she was seeing. "Mr. Staley, you said I could write your story. I can see what you are thinking and that's not fair." Jeff has seen this scenario before. When a person finds out that you're a writer, they want you to do their story. Realizing it would be in vain to try and convince Keeley that he had no intentions of writing Jacobs story, he let it be.

Bill came to the door and shook Jacob's hand. "The turkey is ready to be served. Did Keeley introduce you to Jeffrey?"

"She did and I'm thrilled that I've had a chance to meet a gifted writer." Keeley looked up, way up, at Jacob with tears in her eyes knowing that Jacob was acting like a traitor. Jacob whispered to her, "you're still my writer." She glared at him knowing full well that if Mr. Williams showed any interest in writing his story he would probably turn on her in a heartbeat.

When the three arrived back at the house, Keeley left the car abruptly, still upset. "I apologize for my daughter's behavior, Jeff."

"You don't have to apologize to me. I love Keeley's hunger to write. It tells me, she will be a writer someday and with a little instruction, she'll be good at it." Bill opened the back door and Jeff went in. "What a delicious aroma," Jeff said with a thank you to Lauren, "I deeply appreciate you and your family inviting me."

"Bill and I are thrilled that you're having dinner with us, but it seems Keeley is a little ticked off at you. Lauren couldn't hold back a chuckle, "What happened? She couldn't have your hundred percent attention?" Tracy called, from the living room for her dad and Jeff to have a talk… You better hurry because Everett, Tracy's boyfriend, will be here at eleven-thirty."

Bill led Jeff to the living room, anxious to hear what Tracy wanted to ask him. "Would you sit down Mr. Williams?" Jeff for the first time, felt a little uneasy about coming to dinner. She pointed to the high back chair and he sat. "Dad, you sit on the couch."

"You want me in this conversation, too?"

"Yes." It was obvious, with her tone of voice that the two were in trouble.

"First off dad, when Everett shows up, I want no mention of his job, of what he plans on doing with his life and any other short comings you think he has… understood?"

Bill gestures to Jeff. "I never do those things, I let him do that to himself." Tracy began to pace knowing they were not taking her seriously. "And Mr. Williams, it's your turn." With Bill smiling, it was hard for Jeff to keep a straight face, but he gave her respect and waited for her flogging. "You speak about your son as though he is looking for someone to marry. He doesn't need you to find him a wife. I saw how you built him up to me, thinking I would want him in a split second and he would want me at the same time. Well in my generation, things don't work that way. Parents do not pick the mate for their child. That's the old days… Is that clear?" They both complied giving Tracy no reason for anymore tongue lashings.

The five sat around waiting for Everett to arrive. Bill opened a bottle of wine and proceeded to fill everyone's glasses; first Jeff's glass, then Lauren's and Tracy's. Keeley grabbed a glass off the table waiting for hers to be filled. "Sorry Keeley, you're having grape juice. "Dad! I go to church every Sunday and have wine at communion, so why can't I have some now?" Bill pours her a small amount. She holds the glass up for more. "That's it Keeley, if you're not satisfied you can dump your glass out and drink juice." She sat down looking at everyone displaying a large grin. In her mind, she is the victor.

At one p.m., the doorbell rang. "I'll get it," yells Tracy, jumping out of her chair. Both Bill and Jeff looked at their wristwatches with Bill remarking, "He is always late." Tracy halfway to the door, turns back, "There you go already, dad. He's not even in the door and you're criticizing him."

When Tracy opened the door, Everett rushed in. "It is really cold today." He takes off his overcoat and the two give each other a quick peck knowing that the family is staring at them. Tracy straightens his tie. "You look very handsome in your suit, Everett." "Thank you, Tracy."

Lauren sips the last ounce from her wine glass and stands up, feeling a little light headed. Tracy grabbed his hand and led him over to Jeff. "Everett, I would like you to meet, Jeffrey Williams, our dinner guest. He's a writer." She felt her warm cheeks with her hands. Keeley chimed in, "Boy, if you were any later I would need a nap." Tracy held back responding to the remark, it was just another jibe. Lauren called, "Come on girls let's get the dinner on the table."

"Everett holds out his hand, to shake with Jeff, "You write for a newspaper?"

"No, I write books."

"You mean like, thick books?"

"About three to four hundred pages."

"I think the last book I read was in grammar school and that thing was only about a hundred pages." Keeley placed the string beans on the table while overhearing what Everett just said. She looked at Mr. Williams, shaking her head in disbelief, rolling her eyes.

"Well Everett, some people do not enjoy reading. I understand, fully. There are times when I never want to read another word from a book and just go do things with my hands. Like maybe gardening or building a house or just sitting in a chair and watching television... In fact, I may never write another novel again." Bill gasped with surprise. Keeley heard it, they all heard what Jeff just said and were shocked, except for Everett.

Keeley started to ask why when her dad interrupted her. They all sat down at the dining room table, then Lauren said the blessing. The table was quiet during the meal.

Jeff was thrilled that the Maxwell family invited him, and he was going to go out of his way to help Keeley. Keeley was exploding inside with anticipation of her classmates coming in a few minutes. "Would you like a tour of our home now?" "I would really love to, and I must say, Lauren, that was a fine meal. Your whole family has been a blessing to me." The two left their chairs and went to the staircase with Keeley following.

"Hold it young lady, smiled Lauren, you and Tracy have to clear the table and do the dishes."

"Ahh, Mom, have Everett help Tracy. They should do things together; it'll be good training for when they get married." Everett got up from his chair and began to stack dishes. Thank you Everett, I owe you one. She looked at her mother for the release-of-duty. None came. Okay, Mom I will clean the entire house next week if you let me go on the tour. Her mother smiled and it gave Keely the go- sign to join Jeff and her Dad.

At three o'clock Keeley's friends showed with the many questions they had. They all sat in the living room clustering as close as they could; all addressing him as Mr. Williams. They fired question after question, almost to the point of not letting him even complete his answer to the previous question. Most of their interests sided with Marilyn's writings. Understandably, Jeff's books were more for the older reader.

"I have a question for you Mr. Williams," declared Keeley. "In Mrs. Williams tenth book titled "Rosie the Rabbit" she wrote about how terrible that mother rabbit was and the sadness which the family of rabbits went through. Her previous books were about happy animals who did funny things, and seemed really nice. I noticed in your books a similar thing happened."

Jeff became very quiet. He looked at each kid and asked, "Did all of you feel what Keeley felt?" All the heads were shaking no, but wishing they were nodding yes. Well kids I really should go now. I had a great time and I hope I answered everyone's questions. The group started to moan. Bill stood, "That's it kids, Mr. Williams has to go. He looked at his wristwatch. "My goodness Mr. Williams has been answering your questions for more than an hour and a half." Keeley stayed on the couch, not even saying goodbye. She felt sorry that she'd asked that question which seemed to upset Mr. Williams. Jeff waved to everyone, gave a special thank you to Lauren, and then went out the door with Bill.

CHAPTER 12

For two days Jeff sat in his room at the Holiday Inn gazing out the fourth story window bored out of his mind. He paced the floor barefoot, to the point he was leaving an imprint on the rug. The T.V. volume was blaring just to keep the dead silence from overtaking his brain. It was time to go home, but the weather all over the northeast was so bad that he was not about to take a chance on the trip home just yet. If he was to pick a positive on this trip, it would be meeting the Maxwell's and seeing Marilyn's first home. Out of the ten legal pads he brought with him he was down to two. The rest were waste paper basket material.

Jeff picked up the phone and called the front desk. "Hi this is Williams in room 406. Could I keep this room for another two nights?" The television volume was too loud, so when he reached over to turn it down, the screen showed a woman on horseback; it was Tracy. "I'll call you back in a minute, thanks."

Jeff listened to the news report, but the story was ending so he didn't understand what it was all about. He grabbed the phone book and found Bill Maxwell Law Offices number. He dialed. His secretary answered, "Hello, this is Carol." "Hi, could I speak to Bill Maxwell please?"

"Mr. Maxwell is busy right now so if you give me your name and number I'll give him the message."

"Oh, Okay. My name is Jeff Williams and my cell is… "Hold on, are you the husband of Marilyn Williams?"

Jeff said, "Yes." Carol said, "Oh that's different, I'll put you through." When Bill answered Jeff said,

"Hi Bill, this is Jeff Williams. I just saw Tracy on T.V. What's that all about?"

"An early storm is blowing in over the next twenty-four hours and that won't give my brother a chance to pull his cattle out of the high country on a regular cattle drive. Tracy was on T.V. asking for help from any experience horsemen. The problem is all the rancher's got caught with their cattle in the higher elevations, leaving everyone shorthanded."

"Can I help?"

"I thought you'd left for home already?"

"No. The northeast is getting clobbered with a huge winter storm, so I decided not to leave yet… so can your brother use my help?"

"It's nice of you to offer, but the high country is very dangerous and it's better to leave it to the experienced guys. I would be going, but I have to be in court at 9:00 a.m. tomorrow, and if I'm not there, I will be held in contempt."

"You said you read most of my books; well every experience that I wrote about was about life threatening and true adventures. I lived in Argentina for six months riding with the Gauchos and at the end of my stay, I broke the meanest horse that lived on the Pampas. Plus, I wouldn't be doing this if I didn't feel I could help."

"I'll call my brother and tell him you'll be going, but I advise against it. Show up at 6 a.m., at my place. I have all the gear you'll need, but if my brother finds some cowboys he'll probably say no to you."

Jeff arrived at 5:50 a.m., and tempers were already flaring. The Maxwell brothers, Bill and Jack were having a heated discussion on whether it is worth saving the cattle that are up higher than six thousand feet. Three of the cowboys never showed. They were shorthanded enough that Jeff was now really needed, even if it meant going to the summit with inexperienced help… "I can handle it," declared Jeff. Bill gave his daughter a hug and reached for Jeff's hand. "You guys take care of each other. Lauren gave Tracy a hug, whispering in her ear, "Stay with Mr. Williams, he's smart." For some reason she was more at ease that Jeff was going.

The two pickups, with seven so called cowboys and one cowgirl, towing eight horses in two trailers headed down highway 93. They climbed El Capitan Mountain as far as the four-wheel drive pickups could make it, then it was time to get on horseback. The horses were led out the trailers and before mounting, Jack Maxwell checked the cinches on each saddle. He looked at everyone. "Listen to me. We have just clouds now, but if the weather changes and it looks like the storm is going to hit, head down the mountain. I have about a thousand head somewhere up this mountain, but they mean nothing to me if I lose one of you. Play it safe. I don't want to go home and explain why a life was lost just to save my cattle… You that have cell phones, keep them dry and turned on."

Tracy convinced Uncle Jack that Jeff should go with her, Jack pointed to Dickson Snider, "You go with these two." He was the best cowboy in Montana. The eight rode up to the first gate and separated. Jack and Cecil went to the east around the mountain because if the storm hit they would get it first. Jeremy took the west fork with three men, and Tracy the north fork with Jeff and Dickson.

Jeff was awed by how well Dickson and Tracy rode. It was like the horse and rider were one. Halfway up the mountain

Dickson pointed over at a clump of trees. "I see some cattle near the timber." Jeff was straining to see one cow let alone several. "I'm going to ride over there and if it is just a few, I'll signal that I'm taking them down about 500 feet then I'll join you guys higher up."

Jeff could see about ten, cows and calves, after Dickson flushed them out. In minutes Dickson was back with them. "That was easy. The cow's kept right on going down the hill." The three were nearing the six-thousand-foot level when Tracy gestured to Jeff by pointing, "That's the summit, so another two miles and we're there. "It seems like this was pretty easy." Dickson smiled, "It's almost two thousand feet higher than right here so be prepared for icy footing; the ascent is just as bad as the descent."

It took the three almost two hours to reach the summit, when they did they discovered that most of the thousand head were there. Tracy pulled her cell phone from the saddlebag and called Uncle Jack. She could hardly hear him, but then she moved slightly and she could make out some of his words… "Uncle Jack, we found most of the herd. They're at the summit and we'll start driving them down." The static made for lousy reception. Tracy was squinting her eyes and covering her other ear, trying to understand his words, "I heard him say west a couple of times. What does he mean?" There's a reason why these cattle are bunched up; they know a storm is coming," shouted Dickson. "Let's round 'em up and send 'em down the west trails. That's the fastest way down this mountain."

Jeff looked to the west, but all he could see was a faint image of El Capitan Peak, "I feel a breeze starting to pick up, Dickson." Dickson gave the order, "Let's push these cattle hard, down the mountain." Hurriedly they circled them and forced them to take the south and west forks creating more ways down. Dickson began jamming his horse against the cows, making them crowd down a narrow path. He could see a white wall coming towards them at break-neck speed.

Jeff yelled at Dickson to get off his horse, we can't make it, It'll be here in seconds. The cattle sensed the danger and spooked, ramming Dickson's horse and him up against the huge rock. The wind was beginning to howl, to the point that hearing each other became difficult. The storm was getting stronger, second by second. The snow was falling at near white out conditions. Jeff pulled his reins and saddlebags off letting his horse go. He helped Dickson to his feet but then saw he was not going anywhere with a compound fracture to his lower leg; and he was semiconscious to boot. He quickly pulled the saddlebags from Dickson's horse, yanked the reins off and let the horse go on its own. Jeff screamed at Tracy to get off her horse, grab the saddlebags and pull the reins off. When she did the horse disappeared into the near whiteout and down the mountain.

Tracy came up close to the two of them with her saddlebags and reins. "I didn't pull the saddle."

"No time to pull the saddle, Tracy." She was stunned to see Jeff releasing a tourniquet and reapplying it. "What happened?"

"He must have landed on this jagged rock when the cattle spooked and trampled his horse. His horse got up, but Dickson didn't. We have to work fast while he's unconscious now. He has a deep gash on his forehead and a compound fracture of the leg." Tracy started to set up a lean-to. "Tracy, I can do that, why don't you attend to Dickson?" She knelt down, almost to a prayer position and looked over to Jeff. It was obvious, she was not mentally ready for this. "Okay Tracy, help me with these ponchos and let's form a wind break quickly." The huge rock was a lifesaver, blocking any strays from running over the trio. It took a minute for the make-do wind breaker to block the brunt of the storm, and then it was time for the two to doctor-up Dickson.

The two dropped to their knees, then Jeff pulled his gloves off to begin. Tracy, with gloves still on, was acting more like an observer when Jeff squeezed her shoulder. "You can do this Tracy. Take your gloves off and let's get to work before Dickson comes to. She took a deep breath… "Okay Tracy, remove the tourniquet." They both paused for the blood to hemorrhage, but very little emerged. "It looks good Mr. Williams. No blood means the arteries and veins are intact." Jeff smiled at her with a thumbs up. She set the bone back in line and closed the wound with ace bandages from her saddlebag. The forehead was easy in comparison to the leg. Using the last ace bandage roll and clipping it tight, she gave out an exuberant cheer of surgical success, barely audible over the howling wind. "Mr. Williams, I would never have done this without you along." She hugged him, showing all her appreciation. "Mr. Williams, I owe you, if you want me to meet your son, I will. My mother said that we should stick together on this mountain and boy was she right. If your son is anything like you, I would love to meet him."

"Well, I think I'm going to hold you to that." They lay down next to Dickson to keep him as warm as possible, until the blizzard passed.

The weather was breaking with only about an hour of daylight left, the two had to work fast to get Dickson ready for travel. Jeff traipsed through a foot of new snow to a fence line and pulled an old post out of the ground. He split the redwood fence post to make a splint. Tracy unfastened the reins from the bridle and used them to strap the pieces together on Dickson's leg. "Hey what are you guys doing? Oh, my aching head!"

"Oh look who is waking up, Jeff, it's Dickson, that lazy cowboy himself." Jeff grinned when he heard Tracy call him by his first name. "We've done all the work and now it's time to go home," Tracy teased Dickson.

"What are you doing to my leg, Jeff?"

"I'm putting splints on it so you don't move it… Tracy patched you up."

"Is that why it hurts like hell?"

"You better thank Tracy for the great job she did, because if I had done it your right leg would be walking east at the same time your body would be going north."

"Uhh… Thanks Tracy for not letting Jeff fix my leg. With him it sounds like I'd be walking two directions at once." They began their descent and after a short distance they stopped; the three stared down a rocky cliff. Tears came to Tracy's eyes. "Oh my God, my horse and a bunch of cattle went over the cliff. You saved my life. I've only known you a few days and already you've saved my life. "Come on Tracy, we better get down this hill before it gets too dark."

Dickson added, "You saved my life too, Mr. Williams. If you hadn't told me to get off my horse, I would have ended up falling over this cliff." "Dickson, mother was so right when she said stay with Mr. Williams, he's smart." Jeff smiled, "It sounds like you too are hallucinating. It was your angels guarding you, Tracy. Let's help Dickson get home."

A knock on Bill Maxwell's back door, two days later, brought the whole family to the kitchen except Keeley. Bill opened the door. "Thanks for coming, Jeff, when you said you were heading home this morning, we just wanted to say goodbye."

"I'm just stopping in for a minute to say my goodbyes because I still have to go to the cemetery, then I'll head home."

"I see you still haven't washed your Jag," Bill observed.

"I'll get it washed on the way out of town. I know it looks disgusting."

"Well Jeff, I asked you to stop in so all of us could say goodbye." Jeff looked around the kitchen. It was Jack, the five cowboys and even Dickson with a huge cast on his leg smiling at their new found friend. "What are you guys trying to do, make me get all emotional?" Jack led the way to shake Jeff's hand, as they all said their goodbyes. The six filed out the back door.

Lauren pointed to a large canvas case. "Jeff, I packed sandwiches of all types, breakfast, lunch, and dinner. I have an ice pack at the bottom, so it'll last. When you get to a motel, microwave whatever you want to eat and you'll be good."

Jeff was smiling, "You shouldn't have. It was such a pleasure meeting all of you. I can't thank you guys enough." Tracy, after coming down the mountain was a changed person. It was only two days, but the family could see how different she sounded. Even being unusually nice to her sister, which sort of got on Keeley's nerves, as a major turnaround.

"Keeley isn't home?" Lauren smiled at Jeff, "She is going to be so upset not saying goodbye. She went with the Girl Scouts group for a two-day outing of learning "manners and etiquette. When she finds out you left, her etiquette and manners will be out the window."

Jeff asked Lauren for a sheet of paper, then sat down at the table to write Keeley a letter. "This letter explains what I would like to do for her, so if you will, tell Keeley, I'll be here for a several weeks at Easter time. It's only if her teacher says okay. The letter explains my plan." Jeff stood, "Oh, and by the way Tracy, what you promised me about meeting Josh when we were up on the mountain; don't feel obligated. I won't hold you to that promise."

"You're not holding me to it?" Tracy asked.

"No. Everett is a nice kid." Bill jumped in, "Wait a minute, Jeff. She promised she would meet your son?"

"I'll handle this dad."

"But if you made a promise, you must keep it. That's how we do things in Montana."

"It sounds like you are backing out of our deal, Mr. Williams." Jeff looked at her as if he missed something in the conversation.

"I'm confused here. You want me to make you honor our promise?"

"That is exactly what I am saying Mr. Williams and here is my phone number. You can also relay a message to your son: If he doesn't call me, I'll be calling him." Tracy declared.

"Do you have his phone number?" She asked. Jeff, cracked a smile like he had checkmated her.

"You will have it as soon as I write it on Keeley's letter. Jeff and Bill couldn't hold back laughter while he wrote the number down and handed her the paper with a great hug.

Jeff picked up his food bag and gestured, "You shouldn't have, Laura, but I thank you very much for this. It will save time on my way home." They walked out the door and stood on the landing. Jeff was surprised, "What is this? You cowboys washed my car!" Jack waited for Jeff to take the last step at the bottom, then gave him a strong handshake, "We just washed and wiped some of the crude off just in case you decided not to wash it leaving town… What amazes me, Jeff, is that I've known you two days and it seems I've known you for years. We will all miss you." Everyone waved as Jeff drove out the driveway in his fairly clean car. The Maxwell's felt like they were saying goodbye to someone they had known all their lives.

Jeff was thankful he had made this trip; he had no more second thoughts. He made his final stop at the cemetery. There he sat in the snow between his two loved ones… "Marilyn, if I can't finish your book after I get home, my plan will be to hire a 13-year-old to do it for me, if she's up to it. I'm sorry I have to leave now. I love you guys." He wiped the snow off the stones then left the cemetery for a quick stop in Chicago, on the way home.

CHAPTER 13

Home from Missoula

Jeff was bone tired when he turned onto his street, slapping his face to stay awake. He turned the volume down on the radio and declared, "It's good to be home." Something caught his eye, he squinted for a moment trying to focus on his house. The light to his writing room, was on. He could feel a certain light headiness come over him, a rush of blood shooting to the brain. He pulled into the driveway and saw Josh's Volkswagen bus parked off the driveway.

His first thought; an accident, somebody was killed. His heart was pounding. The yard light went on and Josh came down the front stairs skipping the three steps and hitting ground. "You're late dad."

"What do you mean I'm late? Nobody knew I was coming home tonight. So how could I be late?" "Your girlfriend called yesterday and said that you should get home around noon today."

Jeff said with a chuckle, "So now you think I have a girlfriend? Maybe I'm dreaming this Josh and I'm not really home yet. A lot of time driving may have addled my brain." Josh gave a sigh and reached for the luggage in the trunk. Jeff pulled the canvas bag from the front seat and slung the strap over his shoulder. "You know what is in this bag Son?"

"Dirty clothes?"

"Nope. The Maxwell's packed enough food in here to suffice for a week."

"That's her name, Maxwell, Tracy Maxwell. That's your girlfriend."

"I think I'm missing something here, Josh."

"Well Dad, let me educate you on the ways to commute love. Tracy called me and said she was worried about your long drive home. That took thirty seconds. Then she went on about how you two went to the mountains together. Then she asked me if I liked veterinary school. That was less than twenty seconds. From there she went on… Your dad is the finest man I have ever met in my life, excluding my own father. That went on and on. Then she asks if I had similar traits and named a few that she saw in you."

"What did you say?"

"I said I have both my mother and my dad in me, so it makes me slightly ahead of the parents… She asked if she could call again and I said sure, anytime, I guess." The two carried the luggage into the house and Josh turned in. Jeff sat in the writing room for a relaxing moment digesting his time in Missoula, and cracking a smile about Josh thinking he had a new girlfriend.

Josh was gone early in the morning, so when Jeff got up he checked to see if he'd left a note on his typewriter, which was the norm. Sure enough, there it was, folded neatly in between the keys. Jeff smiled and opened it… *Dear Dad, I was thinking about you and Tracy this morning and it dawned on me that she had a young sounding voice. You wouldn't be robbing the cradle, right? You're always thinking what person would be best for me, so I'm thinking you should know what is best for yourself.*

Love You, Dad... Josh

Jeff sat down at his typewriter, chuckling at Josh's note, then attempted a test run at Marilyn's book. It didn't take long to discover the inevitable; nothing changed. The difference this time was there was less anger or angst. Something was telling him that his new friend, Keeley, was going to make a difference. He took Marilyn's tenth novel down from the bookcase and began to read. This is the one that Keeley said was quite different from the previous nine.

Jeff was so into her book, when Alice left the house and drove out the driveway, he didn't hear a thing, until she started down the street. In just a few hours, Jeff knew what Keeley had discerned about the two writers. This kid knew Jeff's writing style had changed as well as Marilyn's, either for the better or worse, it didn't matter at the time. But, in the subconscious, it had.

Jeff turned his chair to the window and asked a question out loud, `Why didn't Alice toot the horn or yell hello or maybe come over for a second? After all we have not seen each other in a while. She did none of those things, so what did I do to possibly upset her?" He shrugged away the thought, giving way to a relaxing day at home. This whole writing quagmire was coming to a head and it was the best Jeff had felt in many months, so nothing was going to take the wind out of his sails.

He jumped to his feet and declared, "I'm starving, I'm going to finish Laurens food." He pulled a giant burrito from the ice chest, when he swung the fridge door open for a drink, he saw a large post-um note, "Joan and I cleaned your fridge, it was so disgusting it was beyond words. So my suggestion to you is, "never bring home left-overs from a restaurant, it turns to ----." He marveled at how clean the fridge looked. The porcelain has never looked whiter, he told himself, but aesthetic beauty has never put food on the table. Now that the women have thrown away all his old, somewhat rancid food, he had to change his plan. He threw the burrito in the fridge momentarily and headed to town, buying a bunch of T.V. dinners to have in reserve in case his writing went into endless hours. It wasn't important that the food was not the healthiest. Eating was always a chore when Jeff had writing on his mind, and the last thing he wanted was to get hungry with nothing in the fridge.

During his trip to the store he could not get the burrito out of his mind. When he got home that giant breakfast burrito quickly became history, and now he was ready to put words to paper… After a very short time he realized his thought processes had not changed, but this time it didn't matter. He sensed a new direction was working its way to the front of his mind. Much like a detective has a light go off in his head after struggling on a case for months, having failed to see the impending evidence sitting right in front of his face until a secretary at the precinct pointed it out. Keeley would be his evidence finder.

By 5:00 p.m. Jeff made his decision to call the Maxwell's in Missoula and offer Keeley a job. He looked over at Marilyn's typewriter and gestured, "It's the best I could do Marilyn, the thirteen-year-old kid is my only hope." He made the call and spoke with Keeley for nearly an hour. She was overwhelmed with excitement and agreed to his proposal. Jeff could hear her voice trembling with excitement as the two hung up.

Headlights glared through Jeff's window when Alice made her turn into the driveway, taking away Jeff's visual. He rolled his chair across the room, making a rambling sound over the hardwood floor to the window. He sat gaping impatiently waiting for her kitchen lights to go on. When they did, he could see Alice coming to the window. With his giant wave of hello, she closed her blinds with no response in kind.

This was not like Alice, and he was going to find out why. He slipped his overcoat on and headed over there. He went to knock on the back door but then tried the doorknob and it opened. "Hey Alice, you left your back door open." She yelled from upstairs, "I just opened it knowing you'd be coming over." Jeff stood next to the bottom of the banister waiting for her to come down.

"So, I hear you had a great time in Missoula."

"Are you coming down, or are we going to yell at each other the rest of the evening?"

"It would be nice for me to change into something more comfortable, or would you like to just see me come down there nude? You seem to be a lover boy, always chasing women." Jeff was shocked at her outrage. "Why are you so upset with me?" She came out the bedroom door and down the stairs with a huff, passing Jeff and going straight to the kitchen with Jeff matching her stride for stride. "Come on Alice, what's the problem?" Alice leaned back against the kitchen sink. "Are you hungry?"

"I bought a pile of T.V dinners from the store… and thanks for cleaning my fridge."

"You forgot that the note said Joan, also."

"I'll thank her when I see her... now what's the problem?"

Alice thought for a second, trying to find exactly the right words to explain her discontent with him. She wanted to make sure that Jeff had no recourse… She was ready. "I spoke with Josh yesterday." Jeff started to laugh immediately, causing Alice to show even more contempt. "Let me guess. It involves Tracy Maxwell as my new girlfriend, right?" She gawked incredulously at the thought that Jeff could see through her.

"What do you expect. I'm a writer. This is what I do. I know things before they happen because I have an inquisitive mind. I put two and two together."

"Oh, stop!"

"Let me clear the air here. Tracy Maxwell is a twenty-two-year-old women, who I think would make a great wife for Josh. She was dying to call Josh, but she didn't know how to explain why she was calling, so she used her smarts and made it sound like she was enchanted with me, and she played Josh like a fiddle."

"My guess was; she was enchanted with you."

"Now you stop, and what's the big deal if I found somebody?"

"Because Joan has an interest in you and I think you do in her."

Jeff frowned rubbing his forehead, fearing what he might say next could step on some sensitive nerve endings. The long drive from Montana gave Jeff a lot of time to think about life. "Alice, I find Joan with all the attributes that a guy could ask for except one. She is extremely intelligent, she has the body and the looks of a magazine cover model, but she has had a lot of men in her life, if I can put that in the kindness text coming from a man."

"That is so reptilian," sniped Alice.

"I'm sorry for saying that, Alice. I'll try to do better with my words." Jeff stood up to go home. "Is Joan coming home soon?"

"Why should you even care? But, no, she left yesterday, she'll be doing her Christmas Show tapping in about four days then she'll be home for Christmas."

"I wonder if she had time to read my books?"

"Doesn't it seem like you're using her to satisfy your needs, and then when you don't need her any longer, it's adios?

"I don't mean to be insensitive, Alice, I just fear something I say regarding her past marriages, could spell an end to our great relationship."

"Okay, we did discuss the books together. You cannot believe how fast she reads with total comprehension. It was unbelievable. She has a complete summary written up for you. She has devoted herself to bringing you out of this self-destruction mode."

"You're trying to make me sound like, in your words, a reptilian, aren't you?"

"Maybe that's too strong, how about 'disdainful?'" She walked him to the back door, gave him a kiss on the cheek and a hug. "Do you think it would be okay to visit Joan in New York?"

"I think she would love it."

"How come you never remarried again, Alice?" She beamed into his eyes with contempt again, "Where did that come from? Sometimes you ask the dumbest questions!" Pushing him out the door, she went to the living room, turned off the lights, and sat in her recliner to watch through her window what Jeff was going to do at his typewriter, never giving dinner a thought. A short time later she could see Jeff draping himself over the typewriter in apparent disgust. Tears started to seep from her eyes. Little did she know it was just a habit for him to drop his head to think. Without ever admitting it, she was in love with him.

CHAPTER 14

When Jeff woke the next morning, he expected it to be a normal day of trying to write. Not this time. He was more interested in seeing Joan in New York. Jeff, after speaking with Keeley on the phone, came to realize the possibility that with tutoring, Keeley could write about her experiences growing up in Missoula, much like what Marilyn went through. Anyway, he was anxious to see Joan at her work and learn a different side of her. He missed her far more than just her being his psychologist, she was becoming a special friend to him in many ways.

He thought for a moment about going to New York. Should he simply show up unannounced or call her and get a scathing dressing-down like he got from Alice. Hummm, he thought. If she thinks the way Alice does she will refuse to see me, that would make it a wasted trip. Apparently, Jeff's right side brain was ahead of his left, because he grabbed the phone and started dialing. Joan answered on the second ring. Hearing her say hello, instantly shut down his normal verbal skills momentarily, which was becoming a normal condition when she answered his phone calls. Then he began to smile, "May I come to visit you in New York?"

She could hear the smile in his voice and quickly responded, "I would like that."

Jeff was surprised not to get a cold shoulder. "I refuse to drive my Jag another fifty miles for at least a week, so I'll take the bus and arrive at the Lower Manhattan bus station at 4 p.m." Joan was impressed that he already had checked out the bus schedule for New York, or was he just, so into himself, that he knew she would throw herself at him. Oh well, she thought, I'm thrilled he wants to come here rather than wait for me to come home.

"I'll have everything arranged when you get here." Joan's excitement to see Jeff was heightened, to say the least.

It was beginning to snow when Jeff stepped off the bus in New York City. He picked up his luggage and headed for the terminal. "Mr. Williams?" Jeff turned, "Yes."

"Let me have your bags, the limo is this way. I'll take you to the hotel. My name is Amos."

"Which hotel will I be staying in?"

"The Mark. That's orders from Ms. Steele. It's very close to her television show."

Jeff frowned, he was beginning to feel like a kept man. Even when he got to his room the phone rang often for any additional services he may need. He finally told the main desk to stop all calls except for Joan Steele.

It was nearing 7:00 p.m. when the phone rang, taking Jeff away from his news program on the T.V. ... "Hello."

"Hi Jeff. I'm so glad you came. I couldn't be happier… We start taping our Christmas show on Friday so that will give us three days to enjoy New York." Jeff was more anxious to find out what her final thoughts were about Marilyn's book, but decided to leave it be and just have fun. He could hear excitement in her voice. "I'm just across the hall from you in room 401. I hope you don't feel I'm too pushy?"

"Hey, you're the Doctor, you should know how to make things work correctly."

"Yes, but you're the writer who knows his every move way in advance, much like a chess player."

"If I were that good I would have figured out Marilyn's story long ago.

Joan, on the phone, could sense something was different in his attitude. "You sound happy; in fact, you sound very happy."

"I am happy." She hoped his happiness stemmed from him missing her more than making the trip to Missoula gave him.

The three days would begin with Joan's suggestion to eat at the Blue Water Grill and from there the two would ad-lib. They shared a timorous, almost bashful, conversation at the table, leading Joan to order a bottle of champagne. When the waiter brought the bottle and opened it, the two looked at each other smiling. They both were reminiscing about the time when they sat on Jeff's couch, drinking and trying to get the better of each other.

Jeff raised his glass of champagne, "I want to make a toast." Joan waited fretfully for his words. "To you Doctor, for being such a challenge for me. She started to raise her glass. "Wait, I'm not through… And to you, Joan, for you giving me a feeling of being 'whole' again." Jeff was holding his glass waiting for Joan to lift hers. "Well, are you going to raise your glass?"

"You're done toasting? Oh, I'm sorry. I was just thinking about what you said; very pleasing words to hear. May I give you a kiss for that?" Jeff got up and came around to her. He gently kissed her and squeezed her hand. A nearby table of six was watching the whole thing and began clapping their approval. Joan turned to them with a shy smile, "You ought to see him at home, this is just his warm-up." Jeff turned to the table and acknowledged, "I modestly agree with her."

The two got back to their rooms. Joan, eager to have a little more social time, asked Jeff if he would like to come into her room for a night cap. He declined. She gave him a heart-felt kiss on the cheek and went to her room feeling somewhat dished.

The phone rang as Joan was sliding under her, seemingly, double king size bed blankets. She answered, "Hello."

"Do you understand why I didn't go in your room?"

"Maybe it's because you're not the person that the people in the restaurant thought you were?" It was quiet for a few seconds. "I'm that person, Joan, but I'm going to let your beautiful mind figure this one out… good night Doctor, I had an absolutely, great time. See you in the morning, maybe around ten?"

"I'll come across the hall and pick you up at ten. I had such a great time tonight, Jeff. Goodnight."

The next two days went by like a blitz. They were both dreading to see the end of this fun holiday. On Thursday noon, Joan's cell phone rang while they were skating on ice at Rockefeller Center. Seeing the caller on the phone face, she answered intently, but not saying a word. Jeff watched as her face blushed a red hue that was far worse than skating in the cold day's air. When she flipped her phone off, she stood staring at Jeff as though her heart stopped. "I have to cut our day short. Two cancellations for the Christmas Show is going to make me go back to work, now."

"Can I go with you?"

"I suppose you can, but why would you? It gets hectic and nerve wracking." Jeff could see how shaken she was, and it was not a fun sight. The two got to the ABC Studios and took the elevator up to the third floor where the producers of the show were waiting. The minute they stepped through the door there was general panic from everyone at the meeting. They were all speaking at once. Joan's special aide was crying. Joan went over to console her and offered words that shifted the blame from her to the rat of a Psychologists who backed out. She sat next to the aide. Jeff found his place behind Joan against the wall. He listened to the shouts, blaming, and innuendos that were flying across the board table. Finally, after an hour Jeff stood up and walked over to the table. "I'll volunteer to be Joan's guest." The lead producer looked over at Joan, "Who is this guy?"

Joan turned her attention to the producer, "You really don't know who this man is?" The room got quiet. "This ladies and gentlemen, is Jeffrey Williams, my neighbor in Connecticut, moreover, a writer who has over one million published words in print."

"So what? Do you really think he could do things on the show that would be remotely close to what those two professors of psychology could offer?"

"He and I have a special bond." The Producer looked smoothly over at Joan, then to Jeff, "I think I'll go with Jeffrey as a guest on our Christmas Show." The word that came to mind when he saw the two looking at each other: "Conjugation." That should make a juicy format for the show; he thought.

The limo sat waiting for Joan and Jeff the next morning. When they came out of the lobby, Jeff was chipper and smiling. Joan was nervous to the point of not wanting to converse. Jeff repeatedly looked her way, but she conveniently thumbed through her brief case for some needed slip of paper.

"Are you worried how I will answer your questions?"

"No, I'm more worried how I phrase them, and that they don't put you on the spot."

"Don't worry, I've done a lot of interviews." His words were not reassuring, especially because she knew something about Jeff's past that only a psychologist would realize after reading his books. She grabbed his hand when the limo driver pulled to the curb.

"I know too much about you. It'll be poignantly destructive if I blunder. Oh, why did you have to volunteer for this?"

They got out of the limo and Joan escorted him to the Green Room where the other guests were waiting for the show to begin. The three hundred strong audience was already seated and waiting for the program to begin. The director yelled on the set, "We have thirty seconds, quiet please."

Joan stood in the wings waiting to go on stage, feeling a knot in her stomach not unlike the pain of a ruptured appendix. She told herself, repeatedly that she had done this hundreds of times with no mistakes, so what was the big deal this time. I have a Doctorate, she told herself, I'm good at what I do. I've spoken in front of thousands of people and some were even Jerry Springer types." She was speaking aloud without realizing her aide was standing next to her with a worried look.

She felt a nudge from her aide, who showed her fingers crossed to Joan, "It's time to go on." Joan walked out on the decorated Christmas stage to the front of her chair, ready to speak after the thunderous applause. Jeff, from the Green Room, was surprised at such a reception for Joan, even a standing ovation developed from the clapping. Joan's bow brought on more thunderous applause. When the clapping stopped and she began to explain that the two scheduled guests would not be on the show. An "awe" moment came from the audience. Jeff remarked in the Green Room to the other guests, "They can sure turn on you fast, can't they?" "But we have a much renowned guest to take their place. We have with us, on the second half of the show, the award winning author of twenty-seven books, Mr. Jeffrey Williams!"

Half the audience gave a polite applause. Jeff could see the disappointed audience being scanned by the cameras. "Looks like I should have studied psychology if I wanted to come on this show," mumbling to anyone within earshot... No comment from Joan's other guests as they left the Green Room.

When the first hour of the show was ending, Jeff's apprehension was taking hold as he looked to the Heavens, "I may need some help here, Marilyn. You know your husband better than he does himself, so keep an eye on me, huh?" Joan's aide opened the door and signaled Jeff to follow her. It was obvious to Jeff that she was even more worried than Joan.

She stopped Jeff just short of being seen by the audience. He was calm and almost stone-like, "Uh, uh...give me a sentence to say when I first get out there. I need something to begin my train of thought." She looked at him incredulously, "Okay, okay, I'm thinking...Say Merry Christmas, Ms. Steele and Merry Christmas to all of you." Joan glanced over to her aide when the director said 10, 9, 8, 7, and could see a horrified look on her face. Joan gave a nervous smile muttering, "God help me." The director pointed his finger at Joan to roll. "Ladies and gentlemen and families, we have not rehearsed or scripted any part for this next hour. I want you to welcome, a wonderful author and my dear friend, Jeffrey Williams!" Again, the applause was nice, but unenthusiastic.

Jeff's first words were exactly like the aide suggested. Hearing the echo of her words gave the aide chills up the back of her neck, fearing what was coming next. But the fears were put to rest when Jeff in mere moments began to sound more like a co-host rather than a guest. Questions were being fired back and forth as though it was a cat and mouse game. The audience was sensing something that was more than friendship or platonic, maybe even a fond, genuine love for each other.

When the audience was given a chance to ask questions, they went with the premise that the two had fallen for each other. Joan repeated over and over that this was not that kind of relationship, but the questions didn't change, the audience became persistent. Jeff stood up and walked to the edge of the stage. The cameramen were scrambling to get focused. Joan clinched her armrests ready to get out of her chair for fear what Jeff was going to say.

"Ladies and gentlemen, I find it necessary to explain a part of my life that has never been addressed before, not even by me." Joan cringed at the likelihood that his announcement would come back to haunt him in the most personal way. Jeff signaled Joan to join him at the edge of the stage. The stage hands quickly mustered up two folding chairs and placed them behind Jeff as though right on cue. He stretched his hand for Joan to join him. She awkwardly came over and sat next to him tucking in her skirt, trying not to show too much leg. The men in the audience were just being men when they watched her sit.

"Sitting next to me is a dear friend, probably the smartest person I have ever known, I'm going to tell you why." The audience's excitement grew, much like when Jeff started the first chapter in a book and was throwing a hook to captivate the reader... "Some months ago I was introduced, by a special family friend, to Joan. The reason she introduced us was that she felt I was losing my mind.

"Three years ago my wife, Marilyn Williams, a writer of children's books, died." You could see and hear the sorrow from the audience's behavior. "I decided to write a book about her life of writing, and how it developed my love for her from the day we met. It was to be an enjoyable, fun exercise, but that is not the way it happened."

"I began the book a year after her death and for the next pleasurable six months, I wrote. It was the best writing experience I'd had in all my years of writing. But, when I got halfway through, I suddenly had no more to write. You can call it writer's block, or brain freeze. All I can say is; it was destroying me.

"Joan came into my life to explain to me why I was stuck. I suppose she found my case challenging." (He smiled and glanced at her) She scanned the audience nodding her head. "It was extremely difficult to get Jeff to open up, because he didn't know himself what was locked in the subconscious part of his brain."

"Joan was ready to give me a simple diagnosis of what probably took place in my brain."

Joan cut him off. "I think I can word this case in simple and general terms so as not to give you personal exposure. I'll go from here." Jeff stopped her. "No Joan, I need to do this… Joan told me in a taxi cab a few weeks ago that I resented my wife Marilyn, for whatever reason. I could hardly even look at Joan again for making such an outrageous statement." All eyes shifted to Joan. "I gave Jeff notice that I was through helping him, then gave him one last bit of advice, go to Missoula, Montana, where Marilyn grew up and try to get the feel of her life growing up, maybe that would help"'

"So I did… You'll never guess what happened. A thirteen-year-old girl, named Keeley Maxwell, whose family now lives in the house that Marilyn grew up in, was one of my readers. This teenager told me that something major happened in my writing after book number nineteen. Joan read my books when I was in Missoula and I ask her now, 'Did you come up with why I behaved the way I did?"'

"Please, Jeff not in front of this audience!"

"Please, Joan, I need to hear it."

Joan shifted slightly trying to get the courage. "You are going to hate me forever, after I say this." Jeff was not taking no for an answer. Joan's face turned red. "God help me if I'm right, because I don't want to be… The two of you fell out of love." The audience moaned shifting their eyes to Jeff. Joan prayed Jeff would take her analysis and leave well enough alone.

"It is true, we did, but before you start judging us, let me make something very clear. Marilyn and I went through some horrible times when we lost our daughter Jodie in a bus accident. Marilyn fought so hard to repair our lives from the loss. I share equal blame for our actions. If I may give advice to you, the T.V. audience, it is this, give 100 per cent to your spouse and realize that an error in judgement can happen, and when it does it should be forgiven. I wrote a manuscript describing how we can grow our lives from the time we meet to the time we marry, and beyond. It shows how it is better to learn to love one step at a time, and when things change, like personalities or everyday humdrum living, you must adapt. Time changes all of us, but sometimes more for one than for the other spouse."

Joan gave Jeff a hug, fighting back her tears. The director gave the sign to stop taping. The audience gave a standing ovation. The two stood up and bowed, Jeff stepped away to acknowledge that Joan was the deserving one, pointing to her.

The show had ratings that doubled any other show in the daytime viewing slot. The Christmas Show would become the biggest awards getter of all the independent studios. With trailers promoting the show, it was easy to see why this show would become one of the best to hit daytime television.

The producers of the show asked if Jeff and Joan would stay in New York for Christmas and celebrate this special day with the entire production team. Joan left that decision up to Jeff. With some reluctance he agreed. She took him aside to make sure this was fine with him. "Jeff, you do not have to do this. I have to be here, but your family and friends are more important."

"I think, Joan, you are very important to me, and I want to be here with you, for Christmas." Joan would later write in her diary, (I love you, Jeffrey Williams, all the days of the rest of my life.)

CHAPTER 15

The phone had been ringing off the hook all morning. It was Jeff's turn to host New Years at his house, and everyone coming wanted to know what to bring. Josh had earlier called his dad telling him he was bringing a friend. Jeff knew it would be Charlotte, Cheryl, or Cherry or whatever her name was, he couldn't remember, but just said yes. Spinga was bringing all his shop employees; even the hot masseuse would be coming. Spinga's justification for asking her: "We need action at the party."

Alice and Joan had been decorating all morning with streamers, lights, and furniture arranging, but now they were gone, so it was quiet time for Jeff. He picked up the phone, sat in his study and dialed the Maxwell's number. Keeley picked it up on the first ring. "Hello!"

"Hi Keeley, this is Jeff Williams."

"I knew you were going to call today; I just knew it." She was almost in tears. "So, have you been writing?" "Yes, I've made a log of my daily trips to and from school, just like Mrs. Williams would have done. Also, I wasn't sure if Mrs. Williams was big into sports? Like doing things after school."

"She wasn't very good at baseball or basketball if that is what you mean, but she loved to ice skate."

"Perfect Mr. Williams, because I am lousy at those things too, but I also love to ice skate." Keeley's voice was quivering with excitement. "Here is what I'm thinking Keeley, so tell me if it'll work for you. She was holding her breath, "How about me coming out there just after Easter and stay until school is out for you? That will give you and your classmates about eight weeks of my teaching. If that's okay with your teacher?"

"Yes. Mrs. Lipperscant, said any type of program you'd like to do. She would love to have you here. Everything you wrote in your letter to me, before you left for Litchfield, I did. I have been working so hard, because I want you to be proud of me. I asked my dad if I could miss Sunday Mass so I could work on Marilyn's thoughts in Missoula. He said no… but it was worth a shot, anyway."

"Don't overdo it, Keeley… Your teachers name is Lipperscant?"

"That's her name Mr. Williams. I couldn't make up a name like hers." He started to laugh. "You will when I teach you." Keeley was chuckling at the other end. "Are your parents at home?"

"They'll be home in a few minutes. They went to the mission with some coats they collected from church donations."

"Is Tracy there?"

"No she left yesterday. She wouldn't tell me where she was going, which of course is what she does all the time. Sometimes she can be so immature that way." Jeff smiled when he heard her say that. "Okay then, Keeley, you will continue logging what you do every day and I will see you after Easter; and give everyone my love, and that includes your sister." Keeley was getting misty-eyed not wanting to say goodbye as she placed the phone down slowly.

Jeff headed for the kitchen to wrap presents for each of his guests. He always tried to match his guests with a present that fit their occupation or their personal character traits. He saved wrapping Joan's present for last. When he completed Joan's he gave a concerned nod to Marilyn's picture. None of the wrapped presents looked like a professional job, but who would expect any different, certainly not Alice.

Jeff was wearing a white shirt and red striped tie, with a pull over red sweater. This was about as grubby as he would go and everyone knew how he was, so everyone came well dressed. When Joan entered with her sleek black satin dress, it was difficult for Jeff to take his eyes off her. Alice entered shortly after Joan, giving Jeff the feeling the two discussed when to make their entrance.

Then suddenly a large group of people headed by Spinga and Mark Dolittle forged their way through the front door. It was people from the diner, from the grocery store, from the bank, and even some that played golf at the country club. Jeff glared at Spinga, indicating maybe he was the reason for this large mass of people that were not invited. Spinga gave a shout of laughter, "Don't blame me, all I said was that maybe you may have liked Missoula enough to move there, and they all wanted to come to your last party."

"I'm not moving to Missoula, you nut case. Now what do I do about the ones I didn't get presents for?"

"I got it, Jeff, tell them they've been bad and Santa didn't bring them anything this year."

"I'm going to tell them, for all of you that do not get a present, you'll all be given a free massage from Amazon Woman.

"Hey, Jeff, my buddy, would you really tell them that?"

"Yes, I would my good buddy… Jeff hopped up on his maple chair for an announcement. "Ladies and gentlemen, I normally give a present to each invited guest, but I hadn't planned on party crashers, but that's alright because Spinga is giving a free massage to all that do not get a present from me." The five old timers that frequent the diner simultaneously shouted, "We don't need a present. One of them looked at Amazon with wide eyes.

"This is going to be the best present of our lives." Spinga headed for the bar to help Mark and maybe drown out the cost of twenty massages. Jeff got off the chair and walked over to Alice and Joan, concerned that Josh and his girl-friend had not yet arrived. "Josh is late." He started for the study window to see if Josh's Volks bus was out there. Joan scampered over to him. "Josh will be at least an hour late."

"So how do you know this?"

"Well, he called me this morning at eight-thirty and said his date just arrived at his condo and she wanted to sleep for a few hours, then he was going to show her the University Campus; and after that make his way here."

"I don't know why his girlfriend has to tour the campus when she is always around there anyway. But, hey what do I know. He seems to be confiding in you more than me."

"Don't get defensive. He had to call me to see if she could stay at my place for the night. I told him she could stay as long as she wanted."

"At least he is being respectful of me by not sleeping with her in my house."

"He won't be sleeping with her in my house, either." Joan reached for his hand, "Come on Mr. Big T.V. personality, let's dance." It didn't take a minute, to notice how well Joan danced. She had smoothness like Ginger Rogers, although he fell somewhat short of Fred Astaire, but followed her moves easily.

The front door opened and Joan saw Josh and his girlfriend. She stopped Jeff from dancing another step. "Listen to me Jeff, do not turn around. I want you to look straight at me. You have a surprise coming shortly. Josh walked his date over to his dad. "Dad, I would like you to meet my new friend." Jeff starring at Joan gave a humorous remark, "May I turn around now?" She nodded yes, with a huge grin.

When he turned and saw Tracy, his eyes widened, "My God, I don't believe my eyes. How did this happen?"

Well, Dad, we talked on the phone nearly every night for the last three weeks and we hit it off."

"Son, you finally listened to me... Boy would I love to have written a story like this. I can see the whole scenario now." Jeff was so excited, he found it hard to put into words. He directed them to the food and drinks then gave them space. "Joan, would you please dance with me?" When the two came together, she could feel his heartbeat racing. "Jeff, you'd better relax some, before you have a heart attack. Your heart feels like it will pop out of your chest." Jeff started to laugh aloud, almost gasping for air. "You want my heartbeat to slow down and you're holding me this tight? I don't think so." He gave her a quick kiss on the lips. "Do I have mistletoe above my head?" "No, I just feel so good about Josh and Tracy that I'm almost crazy."

"Oh I thought it was more than that."

Spinga was at the bar giving Alice a drink when he tapped her on the arm to take a gander at Jeff and Joan. "I always knew this was going to happen," as he poured her drink. "You're just a romantic at heart, Spinga."

"By the way, Alice, did you see Joan's Christmas Show with Jeff doing most of the talking?"

"I missed it, but I'm going to watch it tomorrow. I taped it."

"You may find something quite surprising. That's all I'm saying." Spinga turned to make another drink for someone, fearing he may have said too much already.

At 2:00 a.m., the crowd dispersed as quickly as they had come. Jeff handed out the presents that the invited guests were promised. He cheerfully advised the rest to make sure and get a free massage from Spinga. Jeff was down to the last present as the last guest left. Josh excused himself so he, Tracy and Alice could carry her luggage to Joan's house.

He and Joan were now alone. Jeff guided her to the very couch on which the two had played the parts of Jeff and Marilyn six months earlier. He handed her the present that might indicate a shirt or maybe a dress would fit into. "I hate to unwrap it, you wrapped it so well."

"You're right, this was my best wrapping job." They both laughed at the gesture. She lifted the box lid to find a manuscript. The title: *A Blue Print for Marriage, by Jeff Williams.* "I can't accept this, Jeff, it's your life's work, this should be for Josh."

"Josh already has a copy, but I want you to have the original."

"Joan, if you really want to understand me, you'll take this gift. But don't think, because it's about my marriage, I shouldn't be giving you this… just the opposite. You are the psychologist and maybe you can see me differently. I think you felt we should have been much more intimate in New York. Take this manuscript and visualize me saying the words. It reads more like a textbook, but if you do what I wrote, over time you will see me as I learned to be, and as I am now.

"This original is a treasure that must be handed down to Josh and for generations to come."

"I'm sorry Joan, I already signed the manuscript to you… too late."

The next morning, Josh and Tracy said their goodbyes. Tracy smirked at Jeff. "When Keeley finds out I was at your New Year's party she is going to have a fit.

"Maybe her manners and etiquette at the Girl Scouts camp will help absorb her feelings."

"You don't really believe that do you?" Jeff leaned in to hug Tracy, whispering, "I'll be the happiest father in the world when you and Josh give me a grandchild." Josh would have been furious with his dad for saving that. She gave him another hug and said goodbye, but not dismissing his wishes.

The two left for the airport, leaving Alice and Joan with the same impression, but Alice had to say it aloud. "Have you ever seen two people that look so much alike? It's amazing, their brown hair, hazel green eyes, their smiles are both the same. They look like they're going on their honeymoon. Soon after, Jeff and Joan went for a jog, hoping to work off all the food and drink from the night before, even in the freezing weather. Alice, all alone, sat down to watch the tape of Joan's Christmas Show. She laughed at the very beginning, the way Jeff and his quiet demeanor stole the audience's heart, and his somewhat nervous expressions displayed. It was exactly like he is at home. But when he announced that he and Marilyn had a fallen out years ago, she was floored. She repeated that line a number of times trying to remember when this period had happened, because she and Sam went through the very same problem. Could the four have gone through the same marriage problem at the same time?

CHAPTER 16

Back to Missoula

The day after Easter was upon them. The Monday that they knew was coming, but had hoped it would always remain tomorrow, was today. Often in those three months after the New Year's party, Jeff couldn't imagine how four husbands could not have seen the beauty of this woman from within. They had to be the worst of marriage material. This gave even more credence on his book "Blue Print for Marriage"

Joan gave Jeff a ride to catch a flight out of Torrington for La Guardia in New York. The short trip was somber, especially for Joan. She'd become so accustomed to having Jeff around all the time, that she knew the days would be boring without him. The two had been attending church together every Sunday and breakfast afterwards. Yesterday they attended mass for Easter Sunday, realizing neither wanted to be separated from the other, but Jeff had made a promise to Keeley, and she held the key to Jeff finishing his book, plus, possibly making Keeley a great writer someday. Joan thought seriously about quitting her television show and going with Jeff to Missoula, but decided it would be best for Jeff to clear these problems on his own terms. She would be a distraction.

He checked his bags in at the terminal and was told it would be twenty minutes to boarding. "Joan, would you like a cup of coffee, I want to talk to you about something." They sat at the table nearest the door to hear the flight number announcements. When the coffee came, Joan reached to take a sip. Jeff stopped her hand and held it. "We don't have a lot of time, so let me get to the point." Joan was fearing, Jeff was never coming back, but didn't know how to tell her. "Would you prefer to write me a letter, Jeff?" (He cracked a grin realizing how well she knew him).

"No, Joan, I have to tell you this in person… I think I'm in love with you. I didn't want this to happen, just like you didn't want it, but I've found myself wanting you near me all the time."

Joan moved to the other side of the table so she could hold him, feeling so relieved. "I know you said that *A Blue Print for Marriage* should stay in the family, well you are my family now. Take the Blue Print and maybe someday, you can actually teach a class on this most important subject. You would be perfect to analyze and teach, maybe high school, and for sure college kids. Hopefully you'll understand, after reading it, if you don't already know, why I acted so cautiously in New York." Joan had already read the manuscript from front to back, but it was going to take a clearer understanding of how a man and woman evolve through years of marriage. Jeff handed her a small wrapped box. "Open this when you get back to your car." He wanted to say more, but the glaring loud speakers sounded for the next flight to New York. Joan held her ears, "So much for sitting at the door so we could hear the intercom. We could have heard it from my car."

They got up from the table, hugged and kissed. "Goodbye Jeff, I'm going to miss you terribly… Call me as often as you can."

"You make saying goodbye seem like a permanent thing. I'll be back in 8 weeks and that means home for good. Besides it will give you time to think about our future together." Joan closed her eyes wishing he would change his mind about going, but knew his commitments would not be compromised.

She left straight for the car while Jeff was boarding. Her mind was on that little box. She sat behind the wheel admiring the homemade bow Jeff had used to hold the lid on. Her tears were losing out to the smiles coming up from her heart. She lifted the lid not expecting a folded note to pop out onto the floorboard. She could feel her heart pounding, knowing that anything he wrote was going to be forever remembered. Joan unfolded the note and she began to read aloud: *Dear Joan, this ring represents everything we've done these past several months. This 14kt. Gold hammered band, shows our somewhat hostile beginning. The wide band shows how we grew in strength together. The aqua marine stone gives me pleasure that someday we will live near the water, which you mentioned, when we first met. On the inside of the band are the words, To Joan, with love, Jeff.* Joan slipped the ring on, it fit perfectly. She looked for his plane, it was gone, even the sound of the engines had faded away.

Jeff's plane touched down at the Missoula Airport at 3:00 p.m. the next day after three flight changes. He was hustling at the counter for a rental car when Tracy tapped him on the shoulder. "You want a lift mister?" He dropped his bags and gave her a big hug. "How did you know I was coming on this flight?"

"Joan called my house this morning and told us. My dad is still at the court house, my mother is in Butte with her neighbor until 7:00 o 'clock tonight, and Keeley is in school, plus she can't drive anyway, it's just you and me, sweetheart."

"It seems as though everyone is worrying about me. Keeping tabs on where I'll be, and when. Not that I don't appreciate it, I do, but I've always been independent. You're spoiling me."

"That's okay, we love you too much not to. So here is plan "A", take you home to stay at our house for the rest of the school year."

"Plan "B" is to not argue with you and to take you wherever you want to go."

"If it won't put you out, I'd like to go to the cemetery, then to the hotel." Tracy drove straight to the cemetery. He was subdued and quiet trying to keep his tears from becoming noticeable, entering the cemetery. When they got to a small birch tree that was just beginning to expose its leaves, he asked her to stop. "I'll wait in the car Mr. Williams."

"Would you please walk with me." The two slipped their jackets on, then walked arm in arm to the graves. They both said a prayer. Tracy moved back, then went back to her car. Jeff walked forward to the two headstones. The afternoon air was brisk with a mild breeze. Jeff stood facing Marilyn's tombstone with hands clasped, "Please Marilyn, forgive me for falling in love with Joan. You would find her fascinating and fun. She is so much like you, a perfectionist, a caring and giving person. I feel like I'm getting back what I had with you. I'm not replacing you in my heart, I could never do that, but I'm adding a great lady. Jody… Give comfort to your mother. I love you both." Jeff walked back to the car hoping not to show tears. "They are both home for good, Tracy".

He gave Tracy a shy smile as they left the cemetery and requested to be dropped at the same hotel where he'd stayed last November. She parked at the hotel entrance and turned off the engine. She could see that Jeff wanted to talk to her.

"Tracy, does Josh speak of his mother and sister when he's on the phone with you?"

"Mr. Williams, Josh and I only call each other when we get lonely. He still has a girlfriend and just because I came to your party doesn't change that fact. I came for you, and of course to see Josh. Before the party, we spoke often leading up to the party, but we both have our own lives."

"Charlotte is not for him. They are not suited for each other. You're perfect for him, unless you don't have an interest in him?"

"I believe her name is Cheryl, and yes, I like him. He is so much like you... At your New Year's party I had the best time with him. I didn't want to leave." Jeff got out and pulled his two suitcases out of the back seat, then leaned forward in the front open window. "Let me see what I can do to change that situation."

"Mr. Williams, sometimes you have to let "Fate" do the living."

"Fate? I don't know the meaning of the word. I make my own directions in life." She pulled his tie bringing his face next to hers, shook her head smiling, and gave him a kiss on the cheek. "You are truly, one of a kind, Mr. Williams." Jeff hurried up to his room to call Joan and give her his plans for the next few days. He was missing her already. The best part of his days would be when he called Joan in the evening and heard her voice.

Keeley had done all the prep work for Jeff to start teaching the writing group, so all he had to do was walk into room 103 and teach. He anxiously walked the twelve blocks from his hotel to the main door of the school, carrying his briefcase with nothing but legal pads that were not even out of their plastic wrap. He opened the main door as though it was fragile. It was the door that Marilyn probably opened hundreds of times to enter the building, he thought. It felt like walking into any other school, but it wasn't. It was Marilyn's grammar school. He followed the classroom door numbers until he got to 103. He could see a crowd of people standing there so he rechecked the door number. 'Huh, it's the right room.' He went in hoping not to find he was wrong… a cheer and applause ensued, catching Jeff totally unprepared. "Is this where I belong?" He asked. Keeley stood up. "Yes Mr. Williams, the adults wanted to see you," she said (rolling her eyes). "Well that's fine." He put the heavy looking briefcase on the desk. All eyes were on it. Jeff smiled as he looked around the room, "Oh, you think I have something important in this brief case? The answer is, I don't; not yet anyway. I carry this case to hold legal pads so that when the time comes I'll have something to write on.

"My purpose here is to teach this writer's group what I know. It could be a lot or it could be nothing, it's up to the student. Now I don't know who everyone is, but my job is to teach these young writers how I write." Mrs. Lipperscant came up to the desk. "Hi Mr. Williams, my name is Mrs. Lipperscant, I teach this seventh grade. If you need any help with anything, I'm available."

"How much time per day do I have with the group?"

"Would a half hour be too much of your time?"

"Could you make it an hour, Mrs. Lipperscant?" She was thrilled to hear Williams wanting more time. "Yes, and thank you for being so generous with your time."

"You're welcome, but it is my pleasure… May I sit at your desk Mrs. Lipperscant?" She pulled back the chair for him. "Yes, of course." She was trying to act with professionalism and not sound like an excited kid.

"Here are the ground rules: You students are the boss. If you want to attend every day, that will be the best approach, you will learn the most. If you find that it's too much work and you can't handle the work load; it will be your choice… Your parents are all welcome to attend class, but no adult questions will be entertained. Only you students can ask questions, because you're the boss. I will not grade you, you will know what you've learned."

"You will learn: How to write a paragraph that will make a reader cry, or how to make a person laugh. You'll discover when you're writing emotionally, it will seem like a roller coaster ride.... And how to know if you have succeeded in those endeavors? The reader should respond with comments like: I cried and laughed and was emotionally drained... Then you know you're on your way."

Jeff was using the distance from hotel to school as his exercise for the day, taking him forty minutes, and having a great workout. The elevation adjustment was especially challenging. After just two weeks, faculty and parents were disappearing. It was fine with the kids and Mrs. Lipperscant. With less distraction in the room, the kids really picked up learning quicker.

Jeff could see that Keeley was in a league by herself. Her negative attitude about slower learners was evident and Jeff had to take her aside and make her understand they all wanted to learn, even the two boys who wanted to be sports writers. She accepted Mr. Williams's words and tried harder to go with the flow. Jeff could see she was trying when one boy asked a question that she considered the dumbest question of the century, and all she did was grit her teeth, a strained smile and clinched fists turning her knuckles white.

The Maxwell's picked up Jeff for dinner as often as he would agree. He restricted his intrusions into their lives to no more than twice a week... One: Going to church and having brunch afterwards, only if they allowed him to pay. Second: Was on Wednesday when their church friends came over to eat and study their faith. He enjoyed those two days of the week because he saw people who really gave a lot of thought to the scripture regarding the afterlife. This was an amazing subject matter for him to research.

On this third Friday of his stay, he needed to find what Keeley had accumulated in notes for Marilyn's book. Keeley was ready and excited for his arrival at seven. At six-thirty, Jeff came down the elevator to the lobby. He went to the vending machine to pull out an egg salad sandwich, then went to the phone at the desk. Merv, the evening manager for the hotel, came out of the back room. "Hi Mr. Williams. I hope your stay has been satisfactory?"

"The service has been excellent. Thank you."

"Are you going out Mr. Williams?"

"Yes, for a couple hours. I'm going to the Maxwell's... would you call a cab for me." Merv reached in his pocket and pulled out his keys. "I can do better than that. Take my car. It's the first one out the door."

"I can't do that!"

"You can and I insist. My daughter Haley is in your class and what you are doing for her is nothing short of remarkable. I've been trying to figure what I could do for you and I finally have my chance. You will use my car anytime you want when I am at work. Now take it."

After an enjoyable dinner Jeff and Keeley sat down at the dining room table to begin the process of editing her notes. He picked up her first three pages from the transcribed notes and began to read. She was showing great strides in writing from her notes, in uniqueness and originality. When he got to the bottom of the second page he started to choke up. "Mr. Williams, would you like a glass of water?" His eyes were tearing. He shook his head no. "I must be catching cold." It wasn't a cold, it was the way Keeley described her walk home one day from school. She wrote: "I was walking home from school alone and was beginning to daydream about the day when I would be leaving for New York to start my writing career." That one sentence made Jeff believe that this kid could possibly become a co-writer to Marilyn's book.

The weather was turning much more agreeable, so Jeff was seeing more people walking their dogs and jogging as he made his way to school. He enjoyed stopping and saying hi, to everyone. His philosophy was simple, anybody that stopped and talked was his opportunity to discover new ideas for the next book. He learned that from Marilyn. Everyone wanted to say something about themselves at one time or another, Marilyn would say. He stressed this to the writers group. "Listen to people more than you talk," he repeated, over and over in class. Your mind will find the words to put on paper from what they say.

On one of his daily jogs to school, he saw Jacob Staley just past the Clark Fork River. He had to make a special stop to talk with this man, even if it meant being a few minutes late to school. Keeley's hopes of writing his story would be challenging, but she had learned enough, in Jeff's eyes, to at least begin work on the life of Jacob Staley.

Jeff stepped across a low fence and yelled at Jacob. "Hey Jacob, may I have a word with you?" Jacob turned around rather visibly irritated at the request, but Jeff came to him anyway. "Hi Jacob, do you remember me?" Jacob frowned, wishing this person would go away. "Hi, I'm Jeff Williams."

"Oh yes, I met you at the shelter. I'm pretty busy right now, Mr. Williams." Jeff kept pursuing his questioning. "Jacob, I've caught you at a bad time?"

"Yes, Mr. Williams, you have."

"May I be of help?"

"Not really Mr. Williams. I've been trying to get these two acres, from the city, to grow vegetables for a farmers' market. I'm measuring the distances from available water to the field and the exact dimensions that we are applying for, then tomorrow I will submit the proposal to the city council. Maybe I could have the homeless work it, then possibly the shelter will be more self-sufficient." Jeff came closer to Jacob. "I think that is a terrific idea. So what can I do to help?"

"Nothing. The city has to approve, and they are reluctant." Jeff reached for his phone to call Bill Maxwell, but the phone had not been charged for several days and was dead. "Have you spoken to Bill Maxwell?"

"He said the city council had not put it on their agenda."

"Let me see what I can do... Now what I wanted to talk to you about was Keeley writing your life story. I would like to see her interview you with me present so I can see how well she converts the interview to paper. Just a short interview for now." Staley had other important issues of the day, rather than worrying about a pipe dream of somebody writing his story. Jeff said his goodbyes to Jacob and the other men, then hurried to class albeit a few minutes late.

Jeff could visualize the whole story that Keeley could write... The city could benefit from the good publicity of letting the homeless become self-sufficient and Keeley would put it all on paper to bring attention through the media. Jeff explained to Bill Maxwell, that his daughter would get a great opportunity to write Staley's story, and still bring attention to the plight of the homeless. A special vote on the subject was brought to the council with the intent it would benefit the community, and a quorum was met, giving the project a reality. Maxwell was amazed at how Jeff made everyone see this project was a win-win, idea.

Word spread quickly about the homeless project, with donations of seedlings from nursery's and money to buy gardening equipment, trickled in. People driving by the patch could see the dedication of hard work put in by these men. Because of that, they began to drop plants off to help the cause. Staley said the morning prayer to the men, before starting the day of work. It was bringing a new meaning to these men and Jeff's spiritual approach.

Keeley was overwhelmed with excitement. She started doing short interviews on weekends, out in the vegetable patch with her note pad and Jeff sitting alongside not saying a word. Jeff smiled at her line of questioning; it was so grown up sounding. Keeley kept looking at Jeff to note the approval or disapproval on his face, as to her line of questioning. No expression came. This was going to be her interview without his help. He would wait till later to suggest some possible changes on interviewing in the classroom.

Jeff glanced around, admiring the freshly planted vegetables, as Keeley conducted her interview. The clear plastic hot caps were covering and protecting them from any sudden morning frost. His thoughts began to wonder. It was like he was in Marilyn's garden, and she was here. "Mr. Williams, are you alright?" Jeff hesitated for a second. "Of course I am, Jacob. I was just admiring how businesses took note of the project and donated supplies of drip lines, fertilizer, and even a gas pump that would bring water up from the river instead of using buckets." It was taking shape just as Jeff had envisioned.

CHAPTER 17

The Rewards of Teaching

"My Darling, what are you doing? You seem to be taking forever to finish my book. Jodie is anxious to read it." "Hi Daddy, I wished for you to write a story about me. Mommy says it's a story about all of us. Is that true?" "Yes, that is true. It is about how we all laughed and cried. I miss you two." "Mommy said we would be seeing you soon."

"Josh talked about how he wished he was older so you two could have played more together. I wrote a little book explaining how all of us loved each other. After he read the book for the first time, he felt much better. He rereads parts of it every time he comes home. I know that, because the book is put back on the shelf, differently. Jodie began to cry. Mommy says I have to go. She says you have to bring Josh here for Mother's Day, she said you would know why."

Jeff jumped up from bed, sweating and shaking uncontrollably. It was so real, seeing them sitting on the side of his bed, He thought. He rushed his shower, deciding he would go to the cemetery. He dressed and went to the large calendar on the wall, showing all the things that had been done on his stay, and what was to be done in the next few weeks. He stepped back remembering all that Jodie said. 'It was just a dream,' he kept telling himself.

He called Joan trying to catch her near the phone. It had been three weeks and the best either could do was leave messages for each other. It was strange not having Joan or Alice answering. He finally noticed that his cell was not plugged in and did so.

He left the room and headed down the elevator to the lobby. When the door opened, he could see Merv working the day shift. He waved to him, at the same time he moved to the exit. "Hold on Mr. Williams, are you going far?"

"Just going to the Coffee Shop, then to the cemetery." Jeff was reluctant to use Merv's car again so he downplayed the long walk down Broadway. Merv wouldn't have it, and gave Jeff his keys. Thanking him, Jeff left, but wished Merv would forget about paying him back for tutoring his daughter.

The Coffee Shop was Jeff's first stop so he could stop his growling stomach. His dreams during the night generated a need for food. He parked next to a car that looked familiar, but passed it off as unlikely. When he passed through the two doorways and entered, he could see that it sure was Bill Maxwell's car because he was sitting in the third booth. The two saw each other instantly and Jeff made his way around the waitress to say hello. Bill got up to shake Jeff's hand. "What are you doing so early in the morning? I thought writer's slept all day and wrote all night!"

"Not me. I'm taking up farming with Jacob. My writing days seem to be in the past."

"Well, I'm sure you'll get it back and be writing more great books… I have to leave to be over at the court house by eight, but Tracy will keep you company." Surprised, Jeff turned.

"Oh hi Tracy! I didn't even see you sitting in the booth. You're the person I wanted to see. I have a plan for you and Josh." Bill hesitated, hoping to hear the plan when they both looked at him, waiting for his goodbye. "Oh, it's between you two?"

When Bill left, Jeff became excited as he began to explain his idea. Jeff quickly ordered breakfast, then asked Tracy if she wanted anything more. Jeff was so excited to see her that breakfast almost became an afterthought. "Tracy, I think I will invite Josh to come to Missoula and spend Mother's Day with me. Of course, that means with you.... So do you think you could show him around town and convince him this is a great place to live?" The food came, leaving Jeff to eat and listen intently at the same time.

"You want me to throw myself on him whether he wants to, or not?"

"Don't put it that way, Tracy. He needs more time with you, then he will know you're the one for him."

"And if he still doesn't see us together after a weekend, you'll give up this cupid contrivance?" Jeff just smiled without answering, blaming his full mouth of food. The two walked out of the restaurant with Tracy clutching his arm, as they neared her car Jeff couldn't resist. "Josh is an outdoors type of guy, so whatever you plan for Mother's Day, keep that in mind, okay?" Jeff wanted her mind to stay on this idea.

"If he comes, I think I know what we could do for the weekend. Of course it all depends on whether he chooses to go with your match making program." Jeff's mind was churning about how everything was going to work as he waved goodbye to her and she waved back. "Hey Mr. Williams, whose car are you driving?"

"It's Merv's at the hotel. He insisted, because, I'm tutoring his daughter at the school, he must pay me back."

Jeff arrived at the cemetery and drove to the budding tree. He sat in the car for a minute thinking how real his dream was, compared to this place He called the final resting place. His heart was beating faster than when he threw his typewriters out the window. It felt strange when he looked at the double headstone with Marilyn's name and not his. He sat down and leaned up against the blank side of the tombstone. "Hello my love. I don't know how I'm going to get Josh to come out here for Mother's Day." With tears streaming down his face began to smile. "I know what you're thinking: You're the big shot writer, now you go figure it out." He looked around at Marilyn's and Jodie's neighbors, the Dunne family was well represented, then his mind came back to his two loves. How terrible would it be not to be buried next to them? He thought. He quickly erased that from his mind and went back to the hotel.

He couldn't get into the hotel room fast enough to check his phone. The charge was enough, so he turned it on. Sure enough, twenty-two messages were registered. He checked the first: "Jeff, when I got home after leaving you at the airport, I had a message from the Surgeons General Office in D.C. asking for help instructing psychologists on how to handle the wounded soldiers coming to a hospital in Germany, from Iraq and Afghanistan. I won't be leaving for seven days so I'll keep trying to call you. Jeff listened to the next two empty recordings. When he tried the button for the third, it was Joan with a message.

"You have probably been trying to call me, but can't get through. The state department didn't want me using my cell phone for incoming and outgoing messages. They gave no explanations why, but someone told me it is precautionary measure so no one could highjack calls and possibly use them against state department policies. Go figure."

"I felt I had to leave you a message on this call before I go to Germany, because it was too important not to say what your manuscript did for me… First off, I want to thank you for the beautiful ring that I will cherish forever, it sent me into tears… Secondly, I am so envious, and even jealous of your insightfulness, perspicaciousness, and savvy ability to write such profound works of love.

"I now understand why you did what you did in New York, when I invited you into my room and you declined. It makes perfect sense now. Every high school senior and college student should have to learn the 'A Blue Print for Marriage' as a prerequisite for graduation. You are so far ahead of us in thought that I have not the words to describe your brilliance, but I can tell you this: I will love you all the days of my life and hopefully beyond."

Jeff put the phone down and moved a chair to the window. He stared at the river below, then scanned the forested trees on the mountains. "God, you have given me two wonderful women to live in my life. You have taken one to be with you, bring back one from Germany to be with me.

Jeff and Mrs. Lipperscant were both waiting at her desk with smiles on their faces as the writer's group filed in. The students were not sure about the smiles, but knew in a few short minutes they would find out. Jeff stood and moved closer to them as they sat. "Mrs. Lipperscant has decided to give all of you a test." Moans broke out, feeling they had been betrayed. Keeley stood, "You said we were not going to be tested and now we are? We are writer's Mr. Williams and you can't test us on our literary prowess."

"What in the world have I created with this class? All of you are sounding like Pulitzer recipients, instead of future winners." He turned to Mrs. Lipperscant, "Would you please tell these writing professionals what the test is about." She handed out the one page criteria on a story and began to read: "You will write a three-hundred-word essay on 'Why Mother's Day is Special?'" You will not have your writing class for five days. You will write this instead.

"It will be going to the top newspapers around the country. They know your story is coming, but they will have the option to print them or not." When the students heard their stories would be sent to major newspapers, they were excited and almost overwhelmed. Mrs. Lipperscant excused the class, then observed that Keeley, Haley, and Kathy were still sitting, probably sharing opinions on how to do this. Jeff whispered to her. "They have already begun the process of putting the story together."

The next five days gave Jeff a chance to work with Jacob Staley in the garden. Jeff showed him how Marilyn did her garden by staking all climbing plants for better production and keeping fruit off the ground. Jacob threw himself into the hard work and long hours, to make this a reality. Jeff was putting everything he had learned from Marilyn into the project, but the lack of sleep was taking its toll on him.

Jacob, at the end of the tomato row, called a fifteen-minute break for the crew. They were no longer addressing each other as homeless. Jacob sat next to Jeff and nudged him with his huge hand. "You look like you're not sleeping enough? Your eyes are getting darker every day. Are you sick?"

"No, I'm not sick, it's just that I'm having nightmares all night long. I can't sleep. One minute it's Marilyn running through my brain, then the next instant it's Joan, the woman back in Litchfield that I miss terribly. I never had this problem when I was back home. I also think it's maybe the fear of flying. Ever since the Trade Center Towers were destroyed by terrorists, I've had this fatal feeling of a similar thing happening on my plane heading home, or Joan's plane flying back from Germany, or even Josh, if he comes to Missoula by plane."

"Whatever is happening to you, you'd better come out of it. These things can screw up your head, I know, I went through it.

Planes are safer and more secure, than they have ever been." Jeff shrugged it off momentarily, then that night in the hotel room, he sat down and began writing his last Will and Testament. This was an annual practice for Jeff, ever since Jodie's accident. His book royalties changed from year to year. This gave him a sense of relaxation, and in turn the best four hours of sleep following the dream he'd had about Marilyn and Jodie several days earlier. When Jeff called Joan, to his surprise, she answered. "Thank God, you're home!"

"It sounds like you really missed me, Jeff." The two spoke for an hour and a half. They both wanted to hear the others voice more than they wanted to speak. At the end of the conversation Jeff told her about writing a will yesterday, she became concerned and upset. Jeff was quick to point out, this was a common practice for him, because of such a big change in income when a new book is published or his past books generate publicity, upping his revenue. But after hearing him talk about how much better he felt, her concerns were lifted. Joan hoped Jeff would dissolve the albatross hanging around his neck, once and for all on this trip, and the two could make serious plans for the future.

The day of reckoning was upon the class. It was Friday and the writing class entered room 103 with the biggest writing challenge of their young lives. Each dropped their three-hundred-word essay folders on Mrs. Lipperscant's desk and sat down. Jeff stood and walked over to the glass bowl that sat on the corner of the desk. All eyes watched the bowl, as Jeff explained, "In this bowl I have nine e-mail addresses of major newspapers across the country, you will each take one. You will email the essay to that address, it will be your responsibility. If you wish, I will look at your essay, but I will not grade them. If I see errors in something that is a no-no, in writing, then Monday and Tuesday I will teach obvious weaknesses that appear in someone's story, but you will not know if it's your article that has a problem or your classmates. I will not tell you where the weaknesses are, just what they are." Jeff sighed, as though it was he who was being put to the test. His goal was that all nine articles would get published before he could call his teaching a success.

"I've wished I had become a teacher all my life," telling the class. "This has been the most rewarding time of my career. It's too bad that two students dropped out, but I think they'll come around, eventually. We have completed almost six weeks and I realize that is a short time, but you students have given your all. I'm so proud of how hard all of you worked. I have seen you grow from mediocre writers to very good writers. With just days left in this class, I plan on easing off a bit after Wednesday. I don't want to burn you kids out. You have the foundation now to become great writers, so the more you write the better you'll become. Now come up and take a rolled up address... And another thing, if your story is not chosen for print, do not get down on yourselves, I've had countless rejections myself. It just depends on who is reading it and how much they don't know. Believe in yourselves, because you are writers. Don't let anyone tell you differently."

The class filed out, picking the rolled up addresses of each newspaper from the bowl. Down the hall you could hear the shouts of joy each had drawn.

Mrs. Lipperscant sat back in her desk chair as Jeff neatly stacked the folders and started to put them in his briefcase. "I was hoping I could read some of them," declared Mrs. Lipperscant.

"We'd be here for two hours, Mrs. Lipperscant. Go home to your husband and I'll read them at my hotel tonight."

"Why don't I give you a ride to your hotel, then we can both work on them, and call me Charmaine, would you please? I am dying to see how well they did."

"Your first name is Charmaine? That is a great first name." Jeff gave in and the two worked for nearly three hours at the hotel taking notes on what they saw that needed work. Jeff had nearly a full page of notes per student. Charmaine marveled at how much he noticed that could be improved upon. She would have given an "A" to all nine students; they were that good. "May I see your notes, Charmaine?" She cringed at the thought, he would be grading her notes.

"Don't think I'm this brilliant scholar that knows everything about writing, because I don't. If I did, I wouldn't have trouble finishing Marilyn's book. Now read my notes and I'll read yours."

When Jeff finished, he wrote at the bottom of page nine: *"You should make the time to write, I enjoy reading the gentleness of your words." -- Jeff.* Charmaine noticed Jeff wrote something. Sitting on the edge of the bed, she finished his notes and laid them on the small table. "You can never tell me you're not brilliant, Mr. Williams, I'm overwhelmed. I have never seen a teacher so driven for the success of his/her students."

Jeff knew he needed Keeley to work toward writing greatness, but it was more. It was an absolute joy seeing students excel beyond their own expectations.

"What time is it anyway?" Jeff reached for his little alarm clock on the table. "Nine-thirty."

"It's late for me to drive home across town. Can I stay here tonight…with you?"

"Please Mrs. Lipperscant, you're married."

"I was married. I've been divorced for a few years. He walked out on me"

"No you can't stay anyway." Charmaine got red faced and started apologizing as fast as her mouth would spew the words. "Charmaine, you don't have to apologize, I know where your heart is and you are a great person, but I have someone back in Litchfield who is very special to me."

She headed to the door quickly grabbing her coat on the way. Jeff went to the door reaching the doorknob before she could. "I think your ex-husband was a complete fool." Jeff leaned in giving her a hug and a kiss on the cheek. "I'll see you in class Monday afternoon." Her red face didn't clear until she left the hotel and walked to her car.

Jeff sat at his table and began to go over the papers again. He couldn't help noticing how well Keeley expressed her words compared to everyone else. He knew she was ready to write Jacob Staley's story and hopefully she'd write the second part of Marilyn's book.

He began to write on his note pad: "I find myself totally grateful to my friends in Litchfield and Missoula, and for this I want to give something that will bring us all together… When Keeley Maxwell writes the Jacob Staley Story she will receive the 'Outstanding Literary Award,' the same one I received many years ago. It is without question, in my mind, that she will accomplish this goal. Joan and I will pay for a trip to New York City for the Maxwell family, Jacob and his girlfriend (if he doesn't have one, he better find one), Merv and his family for being such a fine, kind man at the Holiday Inn. Charmaine and a friend, the writing class of all eleven students, even the two who didn't complete. Maybe it will stimulate them. To my dear friends Carly, Jamie, Alice, Mark, and Spinga, who have put up with my insane moods."

Note # 2: "Josh will have a choice to live in my home, but if he chooses not to, then Alice will have the option to give the home to the girls, Carly and Jamie. Alice will have both their mortgages paid in full. Spinga and Mark Mitchell will get golf memberships to any club, paid for life." Jeff started to laugh aloud, "I love writing a scenario that is way in the future.

Jeff got up from the bed and went to his large calendar on the wall. He mumbled as he wrote, "Call Josh in the morning to discuss coming here for Mother's Day. Call Joan and give her an update on how things are progressing here, maybe more."

At sunrise, Jeff jumped out of bed, preparing to go to Jacob's garden for some physical work. "I can see the future with Keeley writing Jacob's book now, but as she progresses she'll be ready to tackle mine." He told himself. "It is hers to finish, I am done writing."

CHAPTER 18

The Mother's Day Miracle

The student's entered room 103 hardly realizing the weekend came and went already. Mrs. Lipperscant came in and closed the door. The class was dead silent, when she entered, because of the anticipation that in mere moments, Mr. Williams will enter and the day of reckoning would be realized. After ten minutes, Mrs. Lipperscant looked at the wall clock. "It appears Mr. Williams is late. So I will start without him.

"I reviewed your papers with Mr. Williams and I can honestly say, you all got "A's from me." She looked at the clock again. "Mr. Williams, on the other hand, saw weaknesses, but before you start to worry, He was very impressed." The class smiled at one another.

The door swung open, startling all of them, even Mrs. Lipperscant. Mr. Williams was dirty, tired looking and had grass stains on his pant knees. "I just came from Jacob's garden and I'm very sorry for being late. I just got so caught up with how well the plants are growing, that I lost track of time. I know that is a lame excuse, so I will have to make it up to you guys."

He removed his backpack, then handed out their papers along with a copy of his and Mrs. Lipperscant's corrections. "Read all the corrections, on the three pages, because you do not know if it may pertain to your article. We are going to have to work doubly hard till Wednesday. While you do that, I'm going to take my tote bag to the restroom to clean up and change clothes." So much for slowing down their workload, at least until they mail off the three-hundred-word essay. The girl's understood why Mr. Williams carried around so many legal pads, they too were throwing away, words-on-paper, that didn't meet their new standards.

On Wednesday, after countless hours, they were ready to send their revised Mother's Day article to their previously drawn newspaper addresses. Mrs. Lipperscant was still in her embarrassed mode from the last Friday night's proposition. For Jeff, it was like it never happened. She too was making a sincere effort to put it behind her, unless of course, Jeff showed any inclination to the contrary.

The kids anxiously went to the library to transfer their stories from note-pads to e-mail conversions. Their excitement was sky high, when they returned. Mrs. Lipperscant fought back her excitement, remembering she was the adult here, but she also realized without Jeffrey Williams, this whole learning experience, would never have happened. The students streamed out of class cheering and shaking hands with Jeffrey and Mrs. Lipperscant, as they headed out the door.

Keeley was last to leave. She smiled and handed Mr. Williams a folder. "What's this Keeley?"

"It's the first half of "*For the Love of Marilyn*". If you are not happy with it, I'll rewrite it or you can put it in your own words." Jeff was speechless and touched by her dedication. Even with all the work she put in on class assignments, she managed to write the first half of Jeff's book, and still found time to interview Mr. Staley, out in the newly formed garden. Jeff was skeptical that she could accomplish this without major flaws. Mrs. Lipperscant looked at the folder as if to say. "Can I read that." But it was too precious to let anyone read it until he first read it back at the hotel.

When Jeff entered the lobby, he went straight to Merv at the front desk. "Merv, does this hotel have a bottle of scotch somewhere?" Merv gave a great big grin and asked, "Would three quarters of a bottle suffice?"

"Absolutely!" Merv went to the back room and pulled from the bottom drawer, his personal stash. "Would this be enough, Jeff?"

"How much do I owe you, Merv?"

"Not one red cent. That look in your eyes tells me the weight of the world has just lifted off your shoulders. That is payment enough." Jeff pressed the button for the elevator, but without hesitation, ran up the four flights of stairs in mere seconds. Pulled a glass from the bathroom, filled it with scotch and sat down to begin reading.

In a few short minutes Jeff was laughing to the point tears were running down his cheeks. After each page he took a sip of scotch. He couldn't wait to read each sentence. The words registered like Marilyn was popping out of each page. Her upbringing was showing why she acted with so many different mannerisms compared to big city kids. It explained why she enjoyed gardening, and animals of all types. Enough even to write stories about them. As much as Keeley wanted the big city world for her career in writing, she will always have what Marilyn always had; country roots.

Jeff finished Keeley's manuscript and placed it on top of his story to Marilyn. It was finally finished, and by a thirteen-year-old girl no less. Jeff leaned back in his chair and proclaimed, "It is finally over and now I can go on with my life." Jeff took the last swallow from the glass and was ready to pour more when he realized, by raising the bottle, over half of the bottle had been consumed.

"I must be drunk, drinking that much," as he cheered. He started to laugh like a drunk would do. But it wasn't so much his being drunk as it was just being free from the torment of two years trying to finish Marilyn's book.

Jeff sat for a minute then told himself, 'I need to write a letter.'

> *Dear Keeley, I have decided to put your name on Marilyn's book as a co-writer. I am instructing my editor and publisher to this effect. They will be thrilled that the book is done, and forever grateful to you. You have a remarkable talent, but be very careful how you let others perceive you. Stay humble and solid as the good person that you are. Don't let your talent consume your humility. Your Co-writer,*
>
> *Jeffrey*

Jeff slipped Keeley's letter into an envelope, then had motivation to write a second letter.

> *Dear Joan,*
>
> *I write this letter to you so when I see you I will not sound like a bumbling idiot trying to get words to mesh with rhythm and devotion. I make no bones about it, you are far superior to me, but if you will have me, I will be your lover for life. You can equate that to just being together out shopping or to having physical endurance marathons, and to being our very core of strength for each other, to the appreciation of sunrises and sunsets, to the touching of hands, and to feeling the blends of chemistry between us, I want*

to take our need for each other to the very perimeters of heaven.

So I ask you, will you marry me?
With all my love, Jeff

Jeff placed the letter in the envelope and addressed it: Joan. He looked out the window admiring the view of the two rivers flowing into one, and the sun peeking through the timber on the mountain slope. It was always there, but now Jeff could see it clearly for the first time. Jeff flopped on the bed giving way to the alcohol. It took a few wake up days to realize everything was real, and Jeff's life of conflict had changed to one of peace.

The hotel phone began to ring. Jeff answered, "Hello!"

"Hi dad! When are you going to charge your phone? I've been trying to call you for an hour. I lost your number and address for your hotel. I called Alice, but she didn't answer, so I called Joan. She gave me your number at the hotel you're staying in."

"Well son, are you coming out to visit?"

"Yes I'm coming. I've scheduled a flight Friday morning, so that means I should be there around six p.m."

"I'm so thrilled. I didn't think it would be this easy to get you out here."

"I spoke with Tracy about the weekend and she seems to be excited… I like her dad." Jeff was silent. "Ah Dad… I can hear you smiling. I know how you operate. You always think you can write the script for everbody's lives."

"You will not regret this trip, son. It will bring all of us closer together. The Maxwell's are going to love you."

"You sound different, dad. Everything work out for you this trip?"

"Everything is great. Keeley did more than I had envisioned with her writing. I think this book about your Mother will be a fabulous book, thanks to Keeley. The kid is really amazing. Her name is going on the cover with mine… I'm planning to fly home on Monday. Maybe we can fly together. Because I am so apprehensive about flying, I took care of all my personal business. You know how I am about dotting my *i's* and crossing my *t's*. I have feared flying ever since the 9/11 attacks. Everyone getting on a plane, looks like a potential terrorist. I hate thinking that way, and I know it's silly, but I can't help it."

"I hope Joan is one of the personal things you took care of. She is perfect for you."

"You sound like your writing my life's script now, son… I'm going to ask her to marry me. Bye for now… I'll see you Friday." Not waiting for Josh to respond, he hung up.

The next two days Jeff stayed close to Jacob for most of the time, but still helped the girl's at school, although Mrs. Lipperscant learned Jeff's method of teaching and was handling the class well. Jeff showed Jacob whatever bits he remembered about gardening, but he was more concerned how well Jacob would open up to Keeley about his life. The two would have to work together to make this a great story and Jeff was determined to show Jacob how to be a good interviewee. Even if it meant working through Sunday.

Jacob had grown accustomed to having Jeff around. He and the other workers decided to give Jeff and everyone who had made contact with him in Missoula, a very special going away party. It was to be a surprise and Keeley and her mother were to handle all the invitations. Holding it at the shelter would bring more awareness, Keeley insisted. So the venue was decided with no objections from the invitees.

On Friday afternoon, Jeff sat in his hotel room waiting for the call from Josh that he had arrived. Merv had already declared his car was ready for Jeff to use. Jeff checked his cell phone to make sure it was working and had a full charge. His impatience added more to his worry and pacing by the minute. His call to the airlines, for the fifth time, drew a sigh and moan from the receptionist desk. "I'm sorry sir, but the plane had a delay at Kanas City." Jeff apologized for the annoyance and hung up returning to his pacing.

While pacing near the window, his doorbell rang. Jeff double-timed to the door and quickly opened it. "Hi dad, and here of course is Tracy." Jeff stood silent for a second, then hugged Josh. Come in you two. "So here I am, waiting to get your call from you for pick up, and Tracy picks you up instead. Now how is that possible when I just spoke to the airline desk and she said the plane had not arrived yet?"

"With such a small terminal, we bribed the woman to tell you that...We kind of want to write our own scenario of what is going to happen this weekend." Jeff issued a deep sigh of relief and gestured, "I certainly wouldn't want to write a story about you two this weekend and expect it to be followed." Josh walked around the room sensing this room looked a lot like back home in the writing room. Messy. "Why did you get such a large room just for yourself? Have you had invited guests over to use the extra bed?" "I need a big room so I can pace the floor without turning around every three steps." "...Dad, you've stuck tacks in the walls holding up notes and full size papers. You are going to have a hundred holes to fill, before you leave here."

"I know son, Merv down at the desk, knows I'm good for it." The three went to dinner, then Tracy said her goodbyes, giving each a kiss on their cheek. "I'll see you tomorrow morning Josh, I'm sure you two have a lot of catching up to do tonight." Jeff became quiet as Tracy left the room. "What's wrong, dad? I do something wrong?"

"I was hoping that you'd go to the cemetery first before going with Tracy."

"Well dad, Tracy and I went to the cemetery before we came here. She knew exactly where Mom and Jodie were buried. She said she goes there often since she met you."

"I'm telling you son, this girl is the one for you."

"I know dad; I've heard you say that many times. Let's just see where the weekend takes us." Jeff sat at the table with Josh and began to explain all that he had done, including his will. Josh was reluctant to discuss life-ending scenarios, but he listened anyway. The more Jeff made reference to giving things of his away, the more uncomfortable Josh became. He was sounding like such a fatalist, listing all the people he wanted to make heirs to his belongings. With Jeff though, it was just like when he laid the groundwork for a new book. You outlined, to the smallest details, what had to be thought of, so that the mistakes would be limited.

Jeff showed Josh the envelope with Joan's name on it, he looked into his father's eyes. "You wrote a letter to Joan? I'll bet that is some letter."

"I'm going to ask her to marry me, if she'll have me. I told you that on the phone and I meant it. How does that sit with you?"

"When you told me that on the phone, you didn't give me a chance to respond. You were probably afraid of my answer. Well you're wrong, I think you two belong together. She's perfect for you and I can guarantee her answer will be yes… She'll really give you a run for your money on brain power." Jeff smiled with that comment.

"I've been thinking, son, I don't think it would be fair for me to expect Joan to live in my home, so I was thinking maybe you could live there."

"Don't you think maybe your looking ahead too far? I don't know where I'll be going to work, Dad. It'll probably be in a large city. When you have a Doctorates degree in Biological sciences jobs are usually given by big companies, and they're in populated areas." Jeff nodded his head agreeing. Josh showered, then came and sat at the back of his bed. "I have a confession to make, dad: Cheryl and I are no longer a couple, but that does not mean Tracy and I will suddenly become a couple either. I have to be settled in a good job before I think of marriage." Jeff turned his head back to Josh with a grin, then continued working on his will, adding simple, meaningless items for the fun of being right...

"It looks like only five hours of sleep for me until morning, so I'm going to have to sleep fast. Goodnight, dad." Jeff wasn't ready to give up on Josh and Tracy for one minute. "The way I see you two is for you to follow my rules of marriage book and for the two of you become veterinarians. You, a large animal doctor and Tracy handling small animals. Oh, and after that you give me a grandchild." Josh shook his head in disbelief. "Goodnight, dad."

"Goodnight, son, call me in the morning so I can say goodbye to you two."

Josh could hear his dad pacing the floor off and on all night, but always returning to the table to write some more. Josh awoke at seven a.m. showered, dressed and was ready when Tracy knocked lightly on the door. Josh opened the door and they quickly embraced and kissed. Had Jeff seen what just happened, he would have realized that the two were farther along in their romance, even if it was by phone, than anyone knew. Rather than wake his dad, he chose to write a note.

> *Good morning dad, Tracy says good morning too.*
>
> *We'll be back at 4:30 tomorrow afternoon. The Maxwell's like going to church, so we'll pick you up to go to Mother's Day Mass at 6 p.m.*
>
> *Our Love to You... Josh & Tracy*

Josh hoped to meet some of Tracy's friends on this trip, so when he mentioned it to her on the phone, a few days before, she reluctantly obliged, and planned for Josh to meet her cousin, Virginia and her husband David, along with a classmate, Susan, and her live-in friend, Adrianne.

The two got down to the parking lot where the couples were waiting. Virginia's first impression was, "Wow! How tall are you?"

"Six-four," Josh answered. Susan looked at Virginia smirking with approval. "Let me introduce you to everyone, Josh, before I regret agreeing to make this a three couple weekend."

"We're just kidding with you Cuz', but I do have to give my stamp of approval."

"Josh, this is my cousin Virginia whose dad is my Uncle Jeremy, my dad's brother. and her husband David who is far too nice for her." They shook hands, then Tracy went on..." This is Susan, my best friend through high school and her boyfriend Adrian." Josh felt very comfortable with this group and knew this could be a fun trip.

Jeff awoke, sat up, and looked over at Josh's bed. It was made as neatly as if nobody slept there. 'Boy son, (talking to himself) you must take after your mother on neatness, because it sure is not me.' He hurried to the garden, working on an excuse for why he was late. The crew began to laugh when Jacob said, "You're late, I will have to deduct it from your pay." Jeff apologized not even realizing the joke.

Jacob put his hand on Jeff's shoulder, patting it, knowing he was going to miss his friend when he left. The two worked the tomato row facing each other, like they had done so often. This way Jeff could coach Jacob to refresh his life story when Keeley asked the questions. Jeff was relentless in his effort to get Jacob to open up. A number of times Jacob shook his monstrous fist in frustration.

On Sunday Jacob and the crew were excited about the surprise party for Jeff. Jeff looked at all of them as though they were intoxicated. "Come on, this garden is looking like the 'Victory Garden' on T.V., so let's keep going. Four hours into the morning Jacob said, "Enough work for today, let's go home." Jeff was deep in thought as he scanned the entire five acres, recalling when the city decided two acres wasn't big enough. "Marilyn would have loved this project, Jacob." Jacob removed his hat and kneeled; the others followed. Jeff appreciated the gesture, but when Jacob began to say a prayer for Marilyn, he too kneeled.

When Jacob completed his prayer they all stood, except Jeff. Jeff was looking down at his hand. "What's wrong Jeff?" Jeff knew his fate if his body couldn't handle this. Jacob came to Jeff and asked again, "What's the matter with your hand?"

"Jacob, I went to get up and I put my hand on some flowering clover. I got stung twice by bee's. I can't survive two stings." Jacob reached for Jeff's phone and discovered it needed a charge, "Do you have a shot kit?" Jeff shook his head, no. He picked up Jeff and yelled to Tony and the crew to stop a car over at the road, to carry Jeff to the hospital. "I can't breathe Jacob." Jacob was running, as fast as his bum knee, would let him. When he got to the end of the row a car had been stopped by the garden crew and was at the ready to transport Jeff to the hospital. Jacob handed Jeff off to Tony and Peter, then he fell to the ground. His knee couldn't hold his weight. When Tony came to help, Jacob waved him off and yelled, "Get Jeff to the hospital now!"

The couples were nearing the bottom of the mountain laughing hysterically at the antics from the night before. Susan wanted to hear the story again about why all the buttons were ripped off both Josh's and Tracy's shirts. Josh began to explain, "Well, Tracy and I were playing strip poker, but our goal was not to strip. My dad wrote a book on courtship for marriage. In this book he tells how you must grow with each other and not jump into the sack at the slightest whim of lust. He describes the building blocks that makes for a sound, lifelong marriage. You must resist all temptations and grow together."

"You mean if David and I had done what this book describes, then we wouldn't argue as much and maybe we would have grown together?"

"I don't know that Virginia, but Tracy and I talked about it last night and decided to try it. It seems that too many couples end in divorce, so if Tracy and I follow this book and build our enjoyment of each other a step at a time, then love will grow to true love. Does that sound corny?"

"No, I don't think that's corny at all, in fact I think that would be a blessing," remarked Virginia. Adrianne summarized, sporting a smile, "So you rip off anything that does not expose your body? Doesn't that go against the very game of strip poker?" Asked David showing signs of agreement. Susan and Virginia just shook their heads at how unromantic the two sounded. Tracy's cell phone began to ring as they reached their cars. "Hi Honey, are you and Josh off the mountain yet?" "Yes, dad, we just got down, in fact, all six of us are saying goodbye." Bill asked, "Can you come home with Josh?" Tracy was alarmed, "What's wrong, dad. Did something happen to gramma?"

CHAPTER 19

The Gathering of Family and Friends
-Three years later-

Keeley finished packing her bags and headed down stairs. The excitement in the Maxwell household was brimming over. Keeley was becoming a local heroine, but she would always remember Mr. Williams' warning in his letter to her: *"Never let fame go to your head. Stay modest. Maintain your roots from Missoula because it is your home for good."*

Bill asked with frustration, "Is your mother ready, Keeley?" "She said, she was right behind me, dad." Josh came in the back door ready to give some change of plans, "I'm sorry, Bill, but Tracy came down with something, so she went to the doctor for medication that will help her when she flies. We will have to leave on the afternoon flight."

Keeley, hoping the whole family would fly together, nudged Josh on the arm. "What kind of a brother-in-law are you, Josh Williams? You have to tell her to tough it out, and go on with us." Josh smiled at his sister-in-law, realizing she was in full-on excitement mode.

"I'll drop you guys off at the terminal, then I'll call you, Lauren, to let you know how Tracy is and what flight we'll be on."

When Josh got home and saw Tracy sitting on the couch resting, he nestled next to her. "So did the doctor give you something, so you can fly without getting sick on the plane Honey?"

"Not exactly, my loving husband. He said it was your fault that I was sick." Tracy stared directly into Josh's pretty hazel blue eye… "I'm pregnant." Josh sat quietly for a few seconds trying to absorb her words. Momentarily she remarked, "It's not like we haven't been trying, Josh."

"I know, I know, but when you finally hear the words they almost seem unreal… I love you, I love you, oh, I love you so much!"

She smiled firmly, "Let's set the rules right now, Josh. You will not pamper me, nor will you ask how I feel every minute of the day, and we are not going to be constantly thinking up names for the baby, understood?" Josh nodded his agreement to her every word, but not verbally; for Josh, that was like not committing to a one-hundred percent contract agreement, much the same as his dad would do.

The two made their flight to New York City, ending the trip at the Roosevelt Hotel at four in the morning. Tracy was little out of it after taking the prescribed pills from her doctor. All she could think about was going to bed. Josh, on the other hand, was recalling memories from just three years before, when his dad begged him to stay the night at the Roosevelt, but had declined because Cheryl wanted no part of Jeff's company. 'How ironic this all was.'

When they got their door card, the two headed to the elevator and stood waiting for the doors to open. The banquet hall doors, just several feet away, were closed, but it didn't matter. Josh knew every part of the room. It brought more sadness to him than joy. Tracy could feel the hurt that Josh was showing. "Listen to me, Josh, this is not going to be a sad moment in our lives. Your dad would not allow it, so let's keep our hearts and minds enjoying what your dad prophetically wrote.

The elevator doors sounded with a bang and bells went off, waking the two from a traveler's daze. Tracy stepped in and Josh went to press the button for the sixth floor, but hesitated momentarily with a thought, then smiled at Tracy, "The whole Williams and Dunne family are gone except for me, but now I'm starting my own family. I have great in-laws, with wonderful family members. Through them I gained a lot of friends in Missoula, along with what I have in Litchfield. What's most incredible of all, is my wife." She moved up against him. He continued, "I don't believe I needed my dad's book on marriage. You are my special love and my dad was totally right when he said you were the one for me. I love you with all my heart, Tracy, and you're right, let's enjoy the weekend and leave sadness behind." Tracy smiled and they kissed. (She could visualize the same words coming from his dad's lips)

Josh had booked nearly all the entire sixth floor for this event. The noise down the halls, even at eight a.m., was nearly out of control.

Daniel, the hotel manager, knocked on Josh's door, hoping to get a little help with the control this bunch of people. Josh opened the door still half asleep. "Oh, hi Daniel. The two hugged, then Josh invited him in, asking, "Is this a nice visit or did somebody do something wrong?"

"I see you checked in at four this morning, so I'm sorry to disturb you two. Daniel was desperate to get a semblance of order in his hotel.

"Well earlier this morning your two buddies, Spinga and Mark, were making a feeble attempt at singing the Missoula High School fight song with the high schoolers…"

Josh asked, "The chaperones didn't stop them or maybe Mrs. Lipperscant?" Daniel answered, "Nope, they were worse than the kids… But now everything is quiet, because they all went sightseeing. What a relief."

"Do we occupy this whole floor, and did everyone show?"

"There are two rooms down at the other end of the hall that are not with your group, the rest are vacant. To your second question: Joan Steele came in last night, along with Carly and Jamie Orenda and their son. Alice Bates, who was going to stay with Joan Steele, is a no show." "Alice will be here," Josh didn't even hear Daniel say that the girls had a son, but Tracy did and nudged Josh as she yawned, "They have a son?" With so many things going through Josh's mind, it never even registered.

Josh suggested to Daniel, "Could you tell the people down the hall I'm sorry for the disturbance. Ask if they want to come to the banquet tonight, they'll be welcome. Also, Daniel, put two nights of their bill on me. I want everyone from Missoula and Litchfield to enjoy this weekend and party as much as they want."

"This is going to be a gigantic bill, Josh."

"This is the way dad would have wanted it." Daniel did as he was told and when he relayed the message to the two rooms, they responded, "Make all the noise you want. we'll even join you."

Josh had the room numbers for all his guest's so he and Tracy decided to say hello to everyone. At twelve-thirty that afternoon most were still out sightseeing. The Maxwell's were in, so Josh invited them to lunch. Tracy called Joan. She instantly accepted and joined them at the elevator.

The 'girls' came out of their room before the elevator doors opened. Carly and Jamie froze at the sight of Josh. Josh quickly came up to them and gave them both a hug, "So is this your son?"

Carly looked down at her son. "Yes, this is Zackary."

"Hi, Zackary. How old are you Zackary?"

Zachary proudly announced, "Four years old." Holding up four fingers with his left hand.

"What are you carrying?"

"My tablet and pencil so I can write." Josh was amazed and chuckled, "My father was a writer and today we are honoring Keeley Maxwell for her writing. It seems that everyone is getting younger and younger in this writing profession… Why don't you guys join us for lunch?"

Jamie responded with a cautious decline. Josh refused to accept their refusal and insisted they get in the elevator. The elevator began the descent, Josh knelt down and asked, "Zackary, may I see what you have written?" Zackary handed the tablet to him with his timid fingers. Josh raised his eyebrows with surprise because of how Zachary had put his words together, asking, "What do you call this line of words?" "It's called a sentence, and if you make a few lines it becomes a paragraph." Josh smiled in disbelief, then stood next to Tracy whispering, "My sister wrote those very words when she was five. I know because my dad framed her words and put them up on the wall in his writing room. Joan could hear Josh, but never said a word, nor did the girls.

Joan sat next to Josh at lunch and was anxious to talk with him. Josh was also eagerly awaiting, the opportune time to find out how her life has been. When those at the table began making small talk between themselves, Josh posed the first question, "Are you still doing your show in New York?"

"Yes, and I would love to do a show with this group of students that Jeff instructed, with fine success, apparently."

"They would absolutely want to." Joan had planned this show with the producers for some time, in hopes they'd approve an, 'on location' show. It would please her to trace Jeff's tracks in Missoula, much like he did with Marilyn growing up.

Joan smiled, "I also teach a class at Rutgers."

"What do you teach?" Josh asked. The table became quiet, anticipating Joan's words about her challenges.

Her smile instantly changed to sadness, "Your dad gave me his book on, what I call, *The Art of Marriage* and asked me to do something with it." Her eyes were starting to tear up.

"Tracy reached across Josh and grabbed Joan's hand, "Was that called, *A Blue Print for Marriage?"*

"Yes it was. I had to change the name of the manuscript because I submitted the manuscript to the Library of Congress and I would be infringing on copyright laws. I just had to send it to the L of C. It was too brilliantly written not to."

"Your dad wanted me to do a teaching class of his manuscript, so last year I applied for a grant to introduce a new class at Rutgers, it was granted by the Department of Education. I explained in detail what the book described. They examined it and said, go with an experimental class for the fall quarter. I had amazing results." Joan looked across the table realizing everyone wanted to hear what it was all about.

Joan began, "You get the students to 'pair up'. They will be together for the full quarter. They will learn from each other how to be kind, honest, respectful, and a host of other things that make for a happy marriage. The two will delve into each other's heart and mind. Hopefully they will work as one." Bill Maxwell gestured with his hand as if waiting to be called on, "Do the couples actually begin to fall for each other?"

"About one-quarter do have special feelings for their mate. I try to discourage this. At least until they have completed half the book, then they can free their emotions a bit. It is truly amazing how Jeff designed this book to work on marriage. He was such a great man." She dropped her head fighting back tears, stopping her speech. Josh leaned over and gave her a hug. They were both feeling a loneliness that would always be there.

The guests were beginning to file in, anticipating a sad but very special evening. It appeared the round tables were far too many for this occasion, but in just minutes the hall was packed. There were far more dignitaries present, compared with three years prior, when they honored Jeff with his last award. Several politicians attended, to pay tribute to the ending of a one great writer and the beginning of a new young one. Movie stars who acted in a number of screenplays from Jeff's books, were in attendance. Also many publishing giants in the industry came to pay their respects to a man they all admired for his achievements, even though it was his student who would be honored tonight.

Seated at the center main table were: Tracy, Josh and Joan. Then Jeremy Sutton, the editor of most of Jeff's books, sat next to Joan. Benjamin Ford, the publisher, Keeley and Jacob Staley sat next to an empty chair with Jacob's crutches leaning against it. The last vacant chair caused Josh to look around wondering where Alice was, "Joan, where's Alice?"

"Alice is not here," she said. "I can see that Joan, but why? Is she sick?"

"Alice eloped with a gentleman she met at a Title Company when she was transacting a home sale last year. She has been on a honeymoon for over a month."

Josh, was flabbergasted, "But she is like my aunt and I'm like her favorite nephew, so how is it that I wasn't invited to her wedding?" The table in unison sounded, "Because she eloped." Josh sat back in his chair shaking his head in disbelief, "Well Joan, you're the psychologist here, why did she elope all of a sudden?"

"I'll tell you later, Josh." Moans came from the table wanting to hear a juicy story.

A nudge came from behind, startling Keeley, "Can I sit here with you?" Keeley looked at Josh, "Zackary, don't you want to sit with mommy and... mommy?" Tracy gave him a pinch on his thigh, disapproving his choice of words. Josh turned to the girls asking them what to do here. They shrugged their shoulders as if to say, you make the call.

"Okay, Zackary, go get your cushion for your chair and you may sit here." Zackary was quick getting the cushion. And of course, his pencil and note pad. Jacob moved over, then Josh helped him up on the chair. Zackary put the pad and pencil next to Keeley, smiling at her, "You like to write too?" "Oh yes Zackary. Do you like to write?" He politely replied, "Yes, ma'am."

"I'm only sixteen, Zackary, you can call me Keeley." A big grin came to his face.

After dinner Ford stood, "Well Keeley, it's time for the show to begin. Are you ready for my introduction?" She nodded a slow yes.

"Do you think Jacob could go up there with me?" Jacob leaned in front of Zackary, "Keeley, this is your night. And even if I wanted to, those four steps to the stage are too hard for me to climb." Benjamin Ford got up, pushed his chair in, and went to the podium.

"Ladies and gentlemen, my name is Benjamin Ford, owner of Ford Publishing, Etc. I hope you enjoyed your meal... it cost me plenty. Especially with my fellow competing publishers in the room getting a free meal, but over the years I'm sure the cost will balance out."

"Tonight we are honoring the youngest ever, recipient for this award. We in the business call this award 'The Best New Writer of the Year Award' and it is no small matter to earn this. The process begins with a number of editor-readers throughout the country writing in, and voting for their choice. This year the votes were overwhelmingly for Keeley Maxwell, but before she comes up here, I would like to say something personal."

"I never worked with Jeffrey Williams, my editors repeatedly told me to learn what Jeff was all about. I was too busy trying to make money and never spending time getting to know him. It is my loss, because Jeffrey passed away three years ago. It is a loss for everyone who loved fiction. For me, I sat down after his death and read all his books. His works were called fiction, but to me they were so true to life. He was a peerless author, whose thoughts and writings were deeper and more profound than any writer I have ever read. I'm the loser for not having personally known such a talent."

"He mentored Keeley and eight of her fellow students from Missoula Grammar school. They are here at table two. Please stand up students, along with your teacher, Mrs. Lipperscant." When they stood, the applause from the three-hundred-plus in attendance, stunned and, humbled the students. "In just a few short months, he filled the young mines of these talented kids with the very best writing methods; and the results were astonishing. These students were so dedicated that all they wanted to do was write, and Jeff treasured every minute of time he spent with them. My editors said that Jeff felt an even greater need to teach after working with this group of students."

Benjamin signaled for the award statue to be brought out. "Keeley, if you would." He extended his hand for her to come up on the stage." Keeley looked over at her parents, giving them a nervous smile. They gave her a nod with smiles of pride and love. She stood and hugged Tracy, Josh, and lastly, Jacob.

A standing ovation met her when she got to the podium. Benjamin quietly asked her, "Would you like to speak before I give you this award?"

"I would love to just take the plaque and go home...." The crowd laughed and chuckled, overhearing her words over the microphone. Then a hush came over the room. She waited for a second then smiled with tears running down her cheeks, then softly said, "But to not to speak would be disrespectful to Mr. Williams, so I will do my best."

"Mr. Williams probably got more out of us, as far as work and life, than all our other teachers combined. But don't get me wrong, I had great teachers, especially Mrs. Lipperscant... On our second day under Mr. Williams' teaching, he handed us a short, three paragraph story. We were in tears before we even finished reading the sad words. He asked, 'Why are all of you crying?' Monica held up her hand, 'because your story is so sad.' He responded, 'Do you see me crying? No, and the reason I'm not is because I know where the story is going. The next chapter is in my head and it diffuses the pain and makes things all good. Learn to keep your brain ahead of what you write."

"The class had an assignment to write *Why We Celebrate Mother's Day,* and we were supposed to send our article to newspaper addresses that we drew from a bowl. I let my mother read it before I mailed it. She looked at me with her big green eyes and began to tear up, trying to hold back her emotions. She probably never thought I could be so nice."

"Mr. Williams taught us how to write those words, but also said that for your writing to be believable, you had to mean the words. I truly meant those words... All our articles from the class were published in nine major newspapers throughout the country.

This was when all of us realized that his teaching and hard work could possibly, lead us to a writing career."

"Mr. Williams was trying to finish a novel about his wife Marilyn, but couldn't seem to make it work. He asked me if I would take notes of my daily routine, so he would understand what his wife's young life was like living in Missoula. I was to go back as far as I could remember. I wrote down everything I did. Walking home from school, playing sports and or anything else that Marilyn may have encountered while growing up in our small western town, even going on family vacations. Marilyn grew up in the house that I live in today. In fact, I sleep in the same bedroom where she slept. That is how all this came to be."

"He knew my initial goal was to write a story about my friend Jacob Staley, who is sitting at our table tonight. After he read my pile of notes on Marilyn, he decided to ask me to write the first half of his own book. My heart was pumping a mile a minute. I do not know why I said I could, but I did. Mr. Williams was going to read what I'd written the following week, on Wednesday.

"That Sunday I went to church without complaining, and prayed from my heart and soul through Mass. I prayed every night before going to sleep. I even stopped at my church on Tuesday just for extra insurance. Wednesday night came and I couldn't eat or function. He read my words and declared I was ready to interview Jacob Staley for my book. He never said I did well, or that my writing was just okay, he just said I was ready for Jacob's story. He left with a joyful look on his face."

"Jacob was a homeless man. He and Mr. Williams and the other homeless people prepared and planted a vegetable garden on five acres. Every chance I had I went out to the garden with Mr. Williams to interview Jacob while they worked on the plants. After each session Mr. Williams would tell me what I was doing wrong as an interviewer. He never said a word while I interviewed

Jacob. Eventually I had stacks of papers about Jacob from when he was three years old to the present. One thing that stood out from our many interviews was when Jacob said, 'We are all homeless in this world, but when we leave this planet, we'll discover our true home.'"

"Mr. Williams and Jacob were working in the garden, when Mr. Williams stood looking over the large garden and declared, 'Marilyn would be very proud of this project, knowing that soon the sale of their fruit and vegetables would be making money for the shelter.' Jacob kneeled down and the others followed. Mr. Williams kneeled, but after the prayer by Jacob, he started to get up, but he was stung on the hand by two bees. He told Jacob that his body could only handle one sting; two would be more than his body could handle. Jacob had old football knee injuries, but he carried Mr. Williams as fast as he could run, and when he got to the road Jacob collapsed with both knees failing him. With the burden of supporting the weight of Mr. Williams that day, Jacob has gone through numerous surgeries to be able walk again. Jacob gave everything he had to try and save his friend." A roar from the crowd and a standing ovation brought Jacob to tears.

Benjamin wanted to hand out the award, but not on this sad note. He motioned for Josh to take the stage. Josh was reluctant, but then relented. "I find myself not able to go forward with this presentation on such a sad note. Maybe Josh can speak about what it was like being Jeff's son, so we can end on a lighter note… Ladies and gentlemen, I present Josh Williams, Jeffrey's son."

"Thank you so much for the advanced warning, Benjamin," Josh shrugged to the crowd and said, "So now what can I say that is light hearted. When I turned sixteen I asked my dad who was smarter, my mother or him. He said, 'Your mother by far.' "Then I said, here is the way I see it, dad, this makes me two times smarter than you two because I have both of your brains. 'Sorry son, one plus one does not, equal one. You will have to work to increase your own intelligence'"

"My dad went on Joan Steele's television show and broke all the rules that one could on a nationally televised show. It turned out to have been Joan's show's highest rating ever, and also for all networks in New York. That was Dad, just telling the truth. Joan Steele, who is sitting at our table, told me a short time ago she's planning to travel to Missoula and tape a show about this special class of kids. Dad would have thought, that was just the greatest." The kids jumped from their chairs and hustled over to give Joan a hug. Joan needed this as much as the kids wanted to do it.

"My dad had a thing about writing stories for people to help them live their lives the way he imagined would be best for them. He always had trouble with a girl I dated. He felt she wasn't the right girl, for one reason or another. I gathered, he was just being overly protective of me.

"So when he met this woman, named Tracy, on his first trip to Missoula, he could hardly wait to tell me that she was the one for me. Both Tracy and I refused to let him decide our fate. The last night of his life, I spoke to him, (Josh was fighting back his emotions taking a deep breath and then continued) He told me he could see my life in the future. I just wagged my head in resignation, that he would never change.

"He said I should become a veterinarian like Tracy was to be. With me treating the large animals and Tracy caring for the small animals. Well it appears he wrote the whole script for the two of us… Now, we can see his vision fulfilled; I'm a vet for big animals and Tracy, my wife, is a vet for small animals… Oh, and one more thing, he wanted a grandchild. We just found out yesterday that my Tracy is pregnant." Josh looked up to the ceiling and mouthed, thanks, dad. The crowd stood, applauding through tears and cheers.

Benjamin came to the microphone and shook Josh's hand, "Here, Josh, why don't you present your sister-in-law the award. This whole thing is too emotional for me." Josh took the plaque, admired it, and walked to the microphone.

"I have been assigned the duties of presenter. Keeley, I give you this award on behalf of the 'Editors and Publishers of America' and I know you will do my dad proud by taking the award with humility. He would want you to cherish the fact that you love to write, and dream about the next words you will put on paper." The guests stood, giving Keeley a rousing ovation. Most of the editors who did the voting could hardly believe that such a young girl as Keeley Maxwell could write so well, far ahead of her years. It was a testament to Jeffrey Williams.

The hall emptied quickly, leaving the tables of Missoula and Litchfield to digest the eventful evening. Josh stood up, "While we are all here, I need suggestions on what to do with dad's home." Joan responded quickly. "How about Carly and Jamie moving in? You two told me earlier you were moving back to the east coast." Joan knew the story about little Zackary and how he came to be. She privately hoped the story would be revealed to Josh. Joan looked at Jamie, waiting for the two to make a move.

Jaimie stood up and asked if Josh would join them in the lobby. The three left with Zackary staying behind with Keeley. The girls went into detail of that memorable night leaving nothing out. Josh returned, with the girls following. Although he was pale as a ghost, Josh made an announcement: "The girls have agreed to move into dad's house." Joan fought hard to keep her laughter inside when she saw Josh's face.

With room checkout due at one, most everyone had left by eleven. Josh called Joan earlier, to have lunch with him and Tracy, because he had a question for her. She agreed and admitted she wanted to talk to the both of them too. Josh and Tracy met her at the hotel restaurant. Josh made no mention to Tracy about what he wanted to discuss at lunch. After they finished eating, Josh debated whether to pursue his question, or just leave well enough alone.

"Josh, did you want to speak to me about something? Your hesitation reminds me of your dad." "That's what I wanted to talk to you about.... Dad spent a lot of time trying to back track my mother' s years living in Missoula. It seems to me you may be trying to do the same thing with my dad. Is it possible you want to go to Missoula and do a segment for your T.V. show to maybe relive what my dad experienced, just like he did with my Mother?"

"Yes, you're right Josh, you're absolutely right. You see, I was in love with your dad once upon a time, I still am, and will, always be. He left me physically, but he will never leave my heart and soul." Tracy leaned over and gave Joan a hug, both of them fighting back tears.

"That last night in the hotel with dad, we spoke openly about you and my mother. I assured my dad that you were the one for him. It felt good to be telling him that, after all he repeatedly told me that Tracy was the one for me. Now it was time for me to tell him what was right for him, even though, he'd already said he was going to marry you."

"I can honestly say, Dad would never have thrown another typewriter out the window being married to you. That's saying a lot, Joan, because he threw many typewriters out the window when he was married to my mother."

Joan sat quietly waiting for the waitress to clear the table. "I don't know how to tell this to the both of you. When I said your dad will never leave my heart and soul, I meant what I said. I haven't told anyone and I probably will never say this to anyone else." She put her hands on the table palms up. Josh and Tracy looked at each other then back to her hands. I want the two of you to grab my hands. They each grabbed a hand. Then the three waited for a few seconds. Suddenly, Tracy jumped, pulling her hand back. Josh sensed a feeling of joy, that was nearly over whelming. He told Tracy to put her hand back on Joan's hand. A calm came over the three of them. They couldn't speak. It was like a spell overtook them. Tracy pulled her hand back and placed it on her flat stomach. "Somebody was telling me to do that." Then the sensation went away. Josh held his chest trying to relax his heavy breathing.

"What was that Joan?"

"I have this feeling often and it can be your father's guarding angel or it's your father, whichever way you look at it, he is protecting us. Nobody has felt what you both just witnessed. Your father is always with me and I knew both of you would feel God's love."

Joan's cell phone rang. She answered then hung up, "My car is outside ready to take me to a producers meeting about my T.V. show tomorrow. Do you two want a ride to the airport?" They declined.

Josh chuckled, "I have to square this gigantic bill with the hotel." The three hugged each other to the point of never wanting to ever let go. The three wiped their tears feeling a miracle just happened, then Joan walked toward the door. Josh called to her, "Remember, Joan." She turned around, "You are our family forever, and I expect the three of us to be together often." She began to walk again, looking back and waving. Tears of joy were running down her cheeks. She still had Jeffrey Williams with her and now she was sharing him with them.

~THE END~